Bride of the Demon King
Destined Enchantment Book 1

By

Viola Grace

Chapter One

*A*liette stood in the shade of the pillars in the stone hall, and she watched what the sisters at the abbey were watching. She watched the sun going down.

Sister Everett held her hand and patted it. "It is fine, child. He will be here to take you to safety, and you will be out of the demon's grip."

Aliette patted Sister Everett's hand. She didn't need to say that she wasn't afraid. The demon wouldn't hurt her. He needed her. All the books said so. The sisters were afraid of what would come to pass if the current demon lord rose to king, so they were hiding her. Aliette was the demon lord's bride and his only path to power.

She heard the pounding of hooves, and the sisters each kissed her on the forehead before handing her up to the courier that would take her to the next place of shelter.

The man placed her behind him, and she carefully took a grip on his tunic. She was not allowed to touch men for more than a moment. Bad things happened when she did.

"It is all right, mistress, I will get you clear of here before the demon arrives."

She made a small noise, and he kicked the horse into action. They thundered away from the abbey and up toward the crest of the hill.

Aliette turned her head toward the abbey, and she sighed. The sisters were burning her clothing. There was a column of smoke with the occasional bright flicker of flame. Her time at the abbey was being erased. Two years of her life were gone in a flash.

Aliette sighed, and she watched the party of men approach the abbey. It was a small group, and they were still some distance away when the courier crested the hill and took them into the safety of the other side.

"We are going into the woods and cutting across the southern plains, mistress."

Aliette cleared her throat. "I can't. I can't pass the barrier of Lord Harrow's lands. You have to stick to the border."

The rider ignored her and pressed onward. They rode through the woods, and when he would have jumped over the stone barrier between Lord Harrow's land and Lord Meskar's, she was simply plucked off the back of the horse by a spectral hand and settled in the long grasses.

Aliette got to her feet and dusted herself off, waiting for him to realize that he had lost his passenger. She had walked five hundred yards along the barrier before she heard the pounding of hooves again.

He jumped his horse back to her side of the barrier, and he leaned down to help her back into position. "What happened to you?"

"I cannot cross the barrier. I have to be hidden from Lord Harrow from within his own demesne. It is frustrating, I know, but it is my life."

She settled back on the horse and took up her previous position. "Whenever you like, we can proceed."

He nodded and nudged the horse back into action, briefing her about her new hiding place while they went. Her education was about to start, so that was something to look forward to.

* * * *

They had been looking for his bride for eleven years. Harrow's father had thrown up a barrier around their lands to keep the bride in, but it was a lot of ground to cover, even for a demon lord.

Flying would have been a great way to search, but that was a skill that he could only fully activate with age or a bride who was able to bear a child.

The latest tip had come from a pilgrim who stopped at the abbey and was beguiled by the bright laughter of a young girl playing around the hanging laundry. When the girl had shown herself, her crimson eyes were unmistakable, and the sisters had taken her in the abbey itself the moment she was seen. That had been the best lead they had had in a decade.

Harrow rode at the head of his small group of warriors, and his lips quirked in a smile when he saw the military formation of the sisters waiting to confront and defy him.

He pulled up his horse and looked at the blaze in the centre of the courtyard. There were bits of unburned paper and fabric that had yet to surrender to the fire.

"So, Mother, you have destroyed all trace of her. Even her scent is fading in the cooling air."

The mother superior stepped forward, and she inclined her head. "We are not sure of whom you speak, but we are merely burning the possessions of the dead, as is our way."

A slight movement of his hand and two of his men bracketed a nervous-looking sister while the other of his men held the group back.

They backed her toward the fire until she was wincing and tears were forming in her eyes. Harrow dismounted and walked toward the woman, using the seduction aura that came so easily to him.

"Well, little one, you have no child here with red eyes?"

The sister looked to her superior, but the woman was surrounded. "No, my lord."

He smiled. He leaned in and whispered softly. "There is no girl-child of about eleven who has touched your heart and soul, who has made you care though you did not want to."

The sister stared at him with wide eyes, and while her arousal was building, so was her mental image of the girl in question. Aliette was the name, and the girl was just beginning her voyage into womanhood. Her eyes were bright rubies, and her hair was rich mink. The sound of her laughter lingered in the sister's mind, and he nodded when he found that she did not know where the child was headed next.

"Do not worry, sister. She is alive,

healthy, and growing in intelligence and beauty. There are things she should be taught, but I will continue my quest to find her. They are not going to harm her, and that is my primary concern. We will keep looking. She is to be mine, and she will be."

He stepped back and brought the woman away from the flames that were causing her robes to smoulder.

The mother superior pushed past his men and reached for her charge. "Let her go."

Harrow looked to the older woman with a quirked brow. "I have. Very wise to burn the fabric, by the way. That is how I nearly caught up this time. Her last home kept one of her first sewing projects and the blood called me here."

The mother superior scowled at him and took in his features. "You have only come to your power."

"Yes, three months ago. Would you

happen to know why?"

The mother superior and the sisters paled. They knew what had happened three months earlier. That was when their charge began her cycles. He knew why it had happened and acknowledged that as long as his body continued its transformation to full demon lord that his bride was healthy.

He was going to keep searching, but the frantic look for the connection was not foremost in his mind. It was time to build his city and set his century-long reign up for a solid start. He would have everything in place when his bride came to him.

As he gathered his men and rode back to the stronghold, he sighed in relief. At least they didn't kill her. Twenty years earlier, that was the fate of his first bride. This time, she had thankfully been born to those with compassion and hope, not the frenzy of fear that the Demon Lord Feir had fanned when the signs of an impending arrival had flowed in the world around them.

A weight lifted off his shoulders where his wings were beginning to thicken to full strength. When he met his bride, he would be presentable, strong, and he would have a place worthy of her to rule at his side. Aliette. He savoured the name that he had lifted from the sister's mind. He would return to his search in earnest in seven years.

Chapter Two

Emrie finished mopping the brow of her patient, and she smiled. "You are recovering well, Kroth."

He coughed and looked at her with bloodshot eyes. "I feel like hell."

She chuckled and knew that he couldn't see through the veil she wore as a healer. "You will be fine, Kroth. Limmia is already on her feet, and she was nearly dead when your neighbours came to get me."

Limmia blushed and slowly stirred the soup that she had been up preparing at dawn. "I wasn't that bad."

Emrie leaned back and sighed. "Dearling, I had to restart your heart."

Limmia paused, blinked, and kept stirring. "Oh."

Kroth struggled to sit up, but Emrie kept him down with one light hand. "Stay put. You are recovering, you are not healthy."

"Yes, Healer." Kroth lay back.

Emrie got to her feet and brushed her robes free of the crumbs of herbs that she had been crushing before her final potion had been completed. Limmia had needed a far more aggressive treatment than her husband, but his frail, masculine body had had a secondary infection that she had had to treat to keep Limmia from a relapse.

Limmia stepped outside to get some garnish for the soup, and Emrie whirled on the man in the bed. "Stop visiting the village whores."

Kroth blinked and stared. "What?"

"You have passed an infection from yourself to Limmia, and it nearly killed her. Do you care for her so little that getting your cock wet is worth her life? Idiot. I have purged it from both of you, and you have a clean start, but I might not be able to reach her the next time, and the results will be on you."

He blinked. "Can't you also cure the whores?"

She lunged and pinned him to the bed with one hand. "And the hundreds of men who have used their services? I can't cure them all. You are dipping your wick where every man with spare coin has been before you, and the women are paid to like you. Limmia loves you, and she does it for nothing more than your company in her life."

Kroth blinked frantically. "She has given me no children."

"She cannot do so while you are spending your seed elsewhere and bringing home disease that would kill your unborn before it starts."

13

The shock on his face made her remember how young he was. Handsome too, for a farmer.

She straightened while Kroth took in her harsh words. She hadn't had time to spend. Limmia was on her way back from the gardens.

He looked up from the bed. "You are serious."

"Yes. I have healed the damage of the illness, but I cannot return time to either of you. You must begin again with a woman who loves you."

There were tears in his eyes. "I think I can do that."

Emrie nodded. "I think you can as well. If you keep to yourself, you will be seeing the signs of new life in six months."

Limmia came back in. "The signs of what?"

Emrie inclined her head, the grey veil that covered her face dipping. "If you

14

two resume marital relations when you are recovered, a child is a likelihood."

Limmia bowed her head. "I think I am barren."

Emrie put her hand on the woman's shoulder. "You are not. Kroth was ill but did not know it, and now, you are both starting again with clean, if weak, bodies and a new chance."

Limmia clutched the herbs in her hands so tightly that the smell of green filled the cottage.

Emrie turned to both of them. "Give yourselves a week, and when you can resume normal chores, you will be able to have sex again. In the meantime, hold each other every night and bless your partner with kind words and soft touches."

Limmia looked at her husband and blushed. "I don't know how to touch him."

Emrie blinked behind her concealment, sat the wife next to the husband, and gave them a lecture on how their bodies belonged to each other alone. Limmia needed to learn what she liked so that she could tell Kroth, and he needed the same. They had a week to figure out what gave them pleasure, if not why, and then, they would be able to share the practice.

Emrie heard a shimmering sound in the distance, and she blinked. "Is it tribute day?"

Limmia nodded. "It is. We made our tribute to the main hall before we got sick."

Emrie nodded. "Sensible. I have to go. Send someone for me if you need me, but I think I have given you enough to think about. For pities sake, talk to each other. You are in this for life. Make the most of it."

Limmia blinked. "Don't you want some dinner?"

"No. I have to spend the evening in contemplation." She swung her bag over her shoulder and nodded to the two. "Take care of yourselves and each other, and summon me if either of you gets worse."

They were so stunned by her sudden departure that they both simply waved farewell.

Emrie went to her horse and saddled it swiftly, kneeing Mithas in the ribs a little more brusquely than he was used to. He sidled and stepped sideways, snorting his displeasure.

"Sorry, Mithas. I am in a bit of a hurry. It is tribute night, and they are putting posts up on the roads. We have to go."

He gave her an understanding look, and she swung up into the saddle, moving rapidly through the village until she could give him his head and he took off, streaking for the woods where she made her home. There was one road out this way, and it led directly past her door.

In the distance, she could see the tribute ports lighting up on the small roads and byways. A small team manned each magical entry point, and each was set to collect tribute for the demon lord in lieu of high taxation. The guards wanted to record the donation properly, so they would request her veil be lifted. That was problematic.

Mithas drove himself as fast as he could, but just as they were within a few yards of the border with the city's lands, a checkpoint flared into life.

She pulled up on her ride, and she dug through her pack while they approached the checkpoint. If she was careful, and she focused, she could get through this.

Emrie stopped Mithas when the guards stood in her path.

"Healer, it is tribute night."

Emrie pulled out the potion she had selected, confirming that it was the one she wanted by looking at it. "My tribute for the demon lord, a powerful truth potion. My name is Healer Emrie."

One of the guards took the potion, and the other wrote her information down.

"Healer, may we see your face?"

She paused, and Mithas shifted slightly before she sighed and nodded. "Of course. I am not on duty, and you are not my patients."

She wrapped the reins around the pommel of the saddle and lifted her veil with both hands. The men looked at her casually and then gasped and stepped back.

Emrie reached into their minds and removed the memory of her while forcing one of them to scrub out her information as her horse moved past them at a slow and steady pace. Keeping her

19

movements calm and deliberate was how she managed to hold onto the minds of the guards until she was firmly tucked into the woods. When she let them go, she lowered her veil and sighed in relief, taking up the reins again and getting Mithas to take her home.

When she got back into her cottage, she looked around and muttered under her breath. "I hate moving."

She started to wrap everything up and stack them in her well-worn travel containers, but the moon rose high and time passed far more quickly than she counted on. She was forced to her bed, and she would continue in the morning. There was no reason that the demon lord would find her at dawn. He had thousands of gifts to run through. A small potion would hardly cause notice.

* * * *

Harrow was looking over the grand ball-room and the thousands of small items that had been donated. He always took a look before the sorting happened and appreciated what his folk chose to gift him with. He was walking through the tribute from the village of Neemin when a familiar scent curled his nostril.

Harrow focused on the origin of the scent, and he ignored the medicinal undercurrent. *There.* He leaned down and snatched the bottle from the collection, inhaling deeply at the scent that he had been searching for. He glanced at his secretary and snapped out, "Reemor, get me the records and the guards who were collecting near Neemin last night."

Reemor didn't ask, merely bowed and left to get the men.

Harrow looked down at the small bottle in his hand, and he uncorked it. A slight sniff told him it was an exceptionally strong truth potion. His queen was a healing mage.

He must have been lost in contemplation for a few minutes, because when he was next disturbed, Reemor was bringing two guardsmen with him who appeared to have dressed in a hurry.

"Lord Harrow, this is Private Jamis and Private Ledon. They were at the Neemin gate last night. Here is their manifest."

Harrow took the document, and he grinned at the first entry. It was crossed out with black in a frenzy of ink. There was no mention of the potion on the list, so the potion had to belong to the first entry.

"Who was the first person to come through the gate?"

Jamis straightened and brushed back his blonde hair. "It was a farmer named Corskall heading for the southern territories. He left a cask of wine."

Harrow held up the small flask.

"Where did this come from?"

The men looked at each other, and their brows furrowed. Ledon cleared his throat. "That didn't come through our gate."

Harrow was nearly dancing in his delight. He focused on Ledon and pressed his mind. There was a ruby-red bubble over a memory that would not be moved. Harrow prodded at the rock-hard magic, and his senses began to hum to life.

He withdrew from Ledon's mind, and he inclined his head. "Reemor, I need horses and a dozen men. The day is wearing on, and my bride is waiting. I don't want her slipping through my grasp. I may be irritated when I do catch up to her otherwise."

"Yes, my lord. Congratulations on the location."

Reemor left, and Harrow turned to the two nervous men. "Now, how many roads lead in and out of Neemin?"

Ledon lifted his chin. "There is one road out of the village that runs through the southern woods. Outside the woods, it branches into three roads that lead south, east, and west. If you begin at the border of the city lands, you will have the best chance of tracking your prey."

Harrow rose to his full height and opened his wings. "She isn't my prey, she is my bride, and soon, she will be my queen."

* * * *

The light crept over her eyelids, and Emrie bolted to her feet, swaying slightly. "Damn it! I am late."

She set breakfast to warming while she worked packing everything she owned into crates that fit on a cart that Mithas could pull.

She took her hair down, brushed it

out, and pinned it up again, setting her veil in place. She quickly had tea and the toasted bread with jam before she heard the hoof beats approaching her cottage.

"Damn it." She got up, straightened her shoulders, and pulled down her veil, setting her arms in her robe and getting ready to face whatever villager in need was approaching. The fact that there were over a dozen horses out there didn't mean that she wasn't going to answer the door like a professional.

She stepped a few feet back and waited for the knock.

Emrie felt him on the other side of the door. She had only been this close to him once before, and it had been his distraction at being wounded that had let her get away. Concealing her scent from him had been the hardest part.

Despite her preparation, she jumped when the knock sounded. Who knew that fate would make actual noise?

Chapter Three

Emrie opened the door and looked up and up at the demon lord on her doorstep. "Hello, is there something you need?"

He was every bit as intimidating as she had heard. He was over seven feet tall, had skin that was a strange combination of blood and bronze, his hair was a thick midnight blue, and his eyes were a bright, flaring gold that was fixed on her veil.

"There is something here that is mine. I have been searching for it for the better part of a decade. Can you help me?"

She could see through her veil very effectively, and she could see in his eyes that the experience was a shared one. "What are you looking for?"

"My bride."

She lifted her veil and looked him in the eye. The men in the background gasped. "If you are the Demon Lord Harrow, then I am your bride."

His smile showed a great deal of fang. "I am Demon Lord Harrow."

She curtsied deeply. "Then, I am your bride."

He bowed and extended his hand to her. "May I know your name, for it is no longer Aliette?"

"Healer Emrie is the name I wear, though I have worn a dozen in my life." She slid her hand along his, and her skin turned from its pale beige into something softly gold. The ripple moved along her flesh until she felt like she was wearing power on her skin.

"Demon Bride Emrie, it is an honour to bring you to your new home."

"Is that where we are going?"

He lifted her into his arms. "It is. Men, get her things and bring them to the stronghold."

She grimaced. "I am already packed; my horse can pull a cart that carries it all. Why are you bothering with my things?"

"You are a healer, and healers need labs and workrooms." He relayed her instructions to his men, and six of them moved to finish packing her up.

She was being held against his chest, and she welcomed his scent. She had been looking for it all her life.

The massive horse in her front yard could only be his, and as he walked to it, the beast held still for him to mount up.

At no time in the process did Harrow come close to letting her go.

The ride to the city took about an hour, and from there, it was another twenty minutes to the palace.

A few minutes from her cottage he asked, "Why the truth potion?"

"It was the most expensive thing I had with me. It was time for tribute, so that was my offering."

He chuckled and shifted her, so she was sitting upright with her back against his chest. "I deeply appreciate the gift. Without it, I would not have found you."

She sighed. "I had been attending patients in Neemin. They needed some counselling, so I stayed too long. The gate appeared in front of me."

He shivered against her back. "You have lived this close to me for how long?"

She smiled. "Not *this* close. But at my cottage for three years. I moved there when I finished my training at the healers' academy."

"The healer's academy, in my city?"

Emrie grinned. "My caretakers and I

thought that you would not look under your own nose, as it were."

"It was a successful ploy. I do not normally enjoy the smell of medicines."

"I know, it was in your file."

He bent down and whispered in her ear. "I have a file?"

"Several. I had to commit them to memory before it was destroyed."

His hands wrapped slowly around her torso. "What did you learn?"

"Favourite foods, favourite colours, favourite battle tactics, and which of your harem you favour over the others."

He sat up straight. "Damn. I am going to have to dismiss them. I would have done so before I left, but I have chased your shadow before."

Emrie twisted and looked up at him. "Dismiss them? All demon lords have harems. Even the ones with queens."

"My father and mother inherited this land, and when they had me, they clung to each other through each trial of my development. At no time was I taught that it would be acceptable for me to keep other women once I wed. Both my father and mother were very clear on that. The demon lord was a title, but I am still Harrow of Rothfield in my soul."

"What about when you become demon king and your impulses fight to impose your will on the world?"

His hands squeezed lightly. "I will have my queen to hold me in check."

She analyzed the feel of his hands on her and smiled as she looked out at the world between the horse's ears. He was the first man to touch her with interest in his hands that hadn't repulsed her. His instincts might have been set on seduction to ease the burning in his body, but right now, his hands had tender care and careful restraint in them. He was keeping her safe.

Emrie thought about the men who

had grabbed her when she tended women in the brothels and the poorer sectors of town. She had been seventeen when she had accompanied a healer on rounds, and a man in the brothel had ignored the signs of a healer, claiming that she was in costume. That was the event that manifested her knife, and his cut had bled until he had begged forgiveness. He had bled for four days until he had come to the healer's school and knelt in front of witnesses, begging for forgiveness and healing. She gave him both.

After that, there were a few attacks while she was working, but they all ended their cycle of violence on their knees and sobbing as they lost blood for weeks in some cases.

"What are you thinking about?"

"Men and what lengths you have to go to in order to educate them. I am sure you are going to be the exception to the rule."

He chuckled. "I am sure that I am not, but I am willing to learn what it takes to please you."

She was bemused by that but murmured, "I believe I am exceedingly high maintenance."

"I look forward to the challenge." He pressed his chin to her head, and she could feel his chest expand as he breathed deeply.

He brought his wings forward to shield her from the snap of the wind. He surrounded her, and she took her own turn to breathe his scent. This was the moment she had been waiting for. She didn't understand when she was a child, but now that she was grown, she had a better idea of the need to pair with someone and what it meant. If it worked out, it would mean giving up a part of herself, but she would get so much more in return.

Harrow's benefit with her at his side would be power. Her benefit would be to offer her skills to their community, the people who had shaped her even when she fought them. She would bring all she had to her position and help Harrow to his full evolution. If happiness could be gained along the way, she would take it. Knowing that she was where she was supposed to be had already started her on her path.

The horse walked through the city, and the people stopped and stared. Some giggled and some pointed, so Emrie sat up straight and unpinned her hair, letting it cascade over her shoulder to hang low. Her hair was her glory and her bane. She couldn't cut it. It hung nearly to her ankles in surprisingly light waves, but it was impervious to damage. She pinned it on her head to keep it out from underfoot, but now, it was one of the signs of her position.

She looked at each and every face with her ruby-red gaze. She knew her eyes were unsettling, but it also was not a look that anyone could copy without going blind. The sneering populace straightened in shock, and then, they bowed as she and their lord passed.

"Subtle." He shifted slightly. "I am a sincere admirer of your hair."

She blinked and smiled slightly. "So, I am not to lean back?"

He exhaled sharply. "If you would, that would be wise. My self-control is a little thin today."

She fought her grin and kept her back straight and eyes on the growing crowds. Folk were running to alert their neighbours, and soon, lines of well-wishers flanked Harrow's horse.

It sounded like the whole city was cheering by the time they reached the stronghold. "That is encouraging."

"It is not every day that a queen

comes home."

On the steps of the stronghold, the demon lord's court was gathered. Emrie took in the sight of the concubines and had to admit that Harrow had varied taste. The women were also very cold if their nipples were any indication.

Harrow dismounted and then turned to offer her his hands. She leaned into him, and his grip around her waist tightened. She was lifted off and set next to him. He offered her his hand, and she settled her fingers against his.

He nodded to the man with the clipboard, and he said, "Reemor, pension and release the harem. Provide them with large dowries and allow them to leave to any destination they like, under escort."

The women gasped. A blonde rushed forward and threw herself at Harrow's feet. She clung to the dark leather of his leggings and wept. "My lord, please. I don't want to go. This new woman can be allowed into our company without loss of our status."

"Miska. That is not possible. I will not have my concubines and my queen under my roof. It is not respectful."

Emrie waited to see what happened next. If they followed protocol, they could stay but not touch the demon lord again, by his own decree. She would need attendants to help her with her daily tasks, and she would need her own secretary. She would prefer her secretary to be a female, but if they were going to insist on being difficult, she would skip the drama and see them gone.

Miska's hand crept up toward Harrow's erection. Emrie moved so quickly that even Harrow didn't react. She was behind Miska with a hand pulling the bejewelled locks back and her head with it. The queen's blade was at the concubine's throat.

"Now, mistress, Harrow has made his will plain, and I will make it plainer. I will not have the likes of you creeping into his bed after making your home elsewhere. I will not risk disease to myself or my lord. You can take your grabby hands and leave this stronghold, or I will take you out one piece at a time, and no one will want you after I am done."

Emrie blinked at her own savagery. She was a healer by nature, but that woman's hands on her mate blanked her mind and fired up her instincts. He was hers, the blonde had had him long enough.

Miska whimpered and stretched a hand out to Harrow. "Please, my lord."

Harrow crouched and faced his ex-lover. "This is my queen, this is her home. I built it for her one stone at a time. You have known since the day you settled here that when she came, you would go. There was never any possibility of anything more. Your contract stipulated the details, and it was read to you before you signed it."

Emrie tilted her head toward the other girls. "Can any of you read?"

A shy redhead raised her hand. "Yes, Ma'am."

Harrow glanced over. "Tyda. New arrival. She was sold to another demon lord, but he didn't like redheads, so he asked me, and I have taken her in. She is untouched as far as I am aware."

Emrie pulled her knife from Miska's throat and yanked her away from Harrow. "Now, mistress, get your funds and leave, or you will be chatting to the knife again, and I can't guarantee what I will do. Demon queens are very territorial."

Miska sobbed, and Emrie hissed. "Knock it off. If you acted this much in bed with Harrow, no wonder you want to keep such an easy job."

Her mate stood. "Hey."

She waved that off, and the woman scuttled away, hiding behind the secretary.

Tyda looked at Emrie and stepped forward, her gauzy skirts rustling and her chalky skin slightly flushed. Tyda knelt at Emrie's feet, and she bent her head. "I swear service to my queen and will follow her edicts in matter of morals and deportment."

Emrie touched her hair, and something happened. Tyda's skin took on a milky-golden hue, and when she looked up, her blue eyes were amethyst. "I accept your fealty and request that you act as my personal secretary."

Tyda took her hand and kissed the back of it. "I will serve with honour."

"Rise, Tyda, demoness of the queen's court."

Tyda stood. "Thank you, my Queen."

Emrie looked to Harrow, and he was shocked. "You can make a demon?"

She quirked her lips at him. "You mean you can't?"

The world around them erupted with shouting, and Harrow escorted her inside while Reemor took care of the courtiers and the concubines.

There were other things to be discussed.

Chapter Four

Harrow took her to his private study after ordering Reemor to prepare the queen's quarters. Emrie was curious about Harrow, and she looked at the way he arranged his study to learn a bit about him while he left to attend to something.

When he returned, she had noted that he alphabetized his books, had a collection of histories of the demon queens, and a large assortment of magical tomes. She was flipping through a defensive spellbook when he brought a tray of food with a few carafes on it.

"Here is something to eat while we talk. I know you had a bit of a meal this morning, but I never pass up the opportunity to have something tasty nearby."

She paused and then looked at the impish look in his eyes. "That is very funny, but I do wonder how this will work. I have never particularly enjoyed the sensation of touch."

He set the tray down on a side table and turned back to her. "I find that hard to believe. I could feel the start of your interest in the pulsing of your heart."

Harrow walked up to her, and she set the spellbook down. He wrapped one huge hand around her neck and smiled. "There it is again."

She opened her mouth to refute that assertion, and he kissed her.

Emrie had been exposed to clumsy attempts through her veil, but this was not one of those. Harrow warmed her, surrounded her, and cherished her with each slow stroke of his lips across hers. When his tongue slid against hers, she blinked in surprise and clutched at his shoulders.

Her pulse thundered in her veins, and she pushed in close to her demon lord while magic began to curl in her belly and whisper between her thighs. The positioning of the magic was peculiar, and she pulled back. For a moment, his hand tightened on her neck as if he wouldn't release her, but then, his grip relaxed.

He exhaled against her mouth, and his breath was sweet. "Too soon?"

"Unfamiliar. I have only ever heard of sex from parties who needed help. No one has ever described anything like this."

She stroked his chest, neck, and the strong line of his jaw before she reached his horns. They were warm to her touch. He was staring at her as she explored him.

"Why are they warm?"

He chuckled. "I am guessing that the same magic that swirls within my horns is what is causing you distress. When the magic rises, it mimics the natural lusts of the body and then drives them higher."

She ran her hands down his cheeks, feeling the texture of his skin that was slightly denser than her own. "Were you always this colour?"

He shook his head carefully in her grip. "No, I was a simple and slightly horned human with gold eyes when I was young. When you were born, my wings sprouted and my skin darkened. When you started your moon cycle, my horns grew."

He leaned in and whispered in her ear, "And when you had your first climax, unheld, untouched, and alone, I kicked my concubines out of my chamber for two weeks."

Emrie's eyes widened. "I had forgotten about that."

"How did it happen?"

She shivered as he slowly began to circle her. "I do a lot of riding, and I have to dress in a hurry. That particular day, I had to run out to assist a midwife with a stalled birth. I pulled on my outer garments but forgot a layer. The friction of the fabric and the saddle caused the climax."

He was behind her now. "Did you enjoy it?"

"It was startling. It was nearly pain but something else. I had to put it out of my mind and get to work. I was needed."

He slowly moved a hand around her waist, and he pressed his long fingers against her. "Would you care to feel it again?"

She gasped and placed her hands over his as he began to rub at her clit. He lifted her left hand and wove his fingers through hers.

Harrow kissed her neck and slowly ran his tongue along her skin. His fingers continued to rub at her, and the spiral of lust and magic swirled outward again.

She felt the slick honey ease from her as her breathing hitched and staggered. A slight groan and grunt came out of her throat. She blushed. This lacked dignity.

He bit her gently, and the spiral spiked, bowing her back as she gripped his hand and wrist tightly. The high-pitched sound that emerged from gritted teeth was unfamiliar, but he continued to stroke and press at her mound until she buckled forward and pushed at his hand to stop the relentless sensation.

He wouldn't stop, so she leaned to the right and bit his arm. He let go, and she staggered forward, catching herself on the desk with both palms, her lungs struggling for air while her body continued to pulse.

"Was it still a surprise?" He asked it innocently.

She turned her head and flushed when she saw him licking the fingers of his right hand.

"No, it wasn't a surprise, but I wasn't expecting... that."

He smiled wickedly. "Neither was I. I look forward to doing it again when you aren't so heavily dressed."

"This is the uniform of my occupation."

"No, as of today, you are the Demon Queen of Spanel Demesne."

She blinked. Emrie was stunned. He was right. Her time being just a healer was over. "Well, hells."

He chuckled. "Indeed. A change of wardrobe is in your future."

She gave him a dark look. "I am not going to be wearing those flimsy, transparent silks that you had the concubines in."

"As tempting as the idea is, it would be inappropriate. A seamstress will come in a few hours, and you can choose something you consider correct for your purposes."

Her body felt like it was under her control, for now, so she stood up straight and gathered her hair up.

"No, leave it."

She snorted. "It is damned inconvenient, and you already know that I am your queen."

He grinned. "I know it. Why did you take Tyda on as your secretary?"

"She has been raised near a demon lord, and she knows their ways. What we do will not shock her, and now that she is a demoness of her own line, she has the power to choose her own lord when she wishes to."

He moved to her and wrapped a hand around her neck again. "How did you do that?"

"It is my particular gift. It has occurred in queens before. They can create lesser demons from those who are worthy. If they are not worthy, the magic will not shape them."

He blinked. "There is no record of that. Courts have been made up of lesser demons, but their origin is supposedly natural."

"You are reading books about queens, not the diaries of them. It is a different perspective." She smiled. "The propagation queens made courts of the most loyal and trustworthy men. They also kept their own most trustworthy women close and transformed them as well."

"How?"

"The queens give. That is what they do. We give you a sexual outlet—"

"Yes, please." He grinned.

"Hush. Sexual, social, and emotional outlets, we catch what the demon kings spill over. We give them strength, power, stamina, and wisdom. A demon king can only be as good as his queen."

He wrapped his arm around her and pulled her in close. "In that case, I may be in line to rule the world."

A knock at the door brought their attention around. In unison, they yelled, "What?"

Reemor opened the door, and he cleared his throat. "With the harem dismantled, where will Miss Tyda reside?"

Emrie answered. "How large are the queen's quarters?"

"A bedchamber, a dressing room, and a study."

She frowned. "Is there a room next to mine that is not occupied?"

"Yes. There is a guest chamber."

She smiled. "Wonderful. Air it out and put her there. When the women have left, I will take a look at the harem and tell you what my plans are for the space."

Reemor blinked and looked at Harrow. "My lord?"

"Do as she says. This is her home now, and she will shape it to her purpose."

Reemor looked startled as if he thought that Horrow wouldn't carry through with his promise. "Yes, my lord."

When the retainer left, Emrie looked up at Harrow. "He isn't going to like me very much."

"He is used to women who fawn over me, not to those who are emotionally mature."

She grinned. "I never fawn. I do look forward to exploring you thoroughly. There might be a few looks of admiration there."

He chuckled and raised his brows. "Would you like me to strip here? I will gladly do it."

She placed a hand on his chest and measured the beats of his heart. "I know you will. You are giddy with discovery today, but I have been planning for this moment since I was a child."

His golden eyes grew wide, and he looked a little embarrassed. "This moment?"

She laughed. "The moment when I was with you."

He ran his hands down her back. "You weren't scared?"

"No. My guardians had the luxury of being terrified, but whatever made me, made me for you, and you for me. We were always a set, which needed each other to reach our goals. Now we can."

He smiled wryly. "You don't even know what my goals are."

"I know that you do the best for your people. The city is clean, the villages are well tended and have their own basic wells and sanitation. These are not things that a careless or angry lord provides." She tapped her fingers on his chest.

"Can you make me fly?"

The question came out of nowhere. "Why?"

"Because these wings are only useful for gliding and short-range hops, and weapons. Flying is my dream."

She blushed and tried not to look at him. "You will be able to fly under some very specific conditions."

He put a finger under her chin and lifted it, so she faced him. "What would make you blush at this point?"

"Pregnancy. I would have to be carrying the next generation for your wings to evolve for that purpose. It will also make you larger and turn you into a complete demon king and me a breeding queen."

He leaned back. "I thought demon kings were sterile."

She cocked her head. "That is truth

and a lie. Most are sterile because they take weak queens. She has been raised to only know what he thinks she should and therefore has no proper sense of self. Her body has no power. These queens haven't even developed their defensive weapons, and that is the first thing that you do when you are threatened."

"How did you develop your weapon?"

She smirked. "I was seventeen, and it was a rapist in a brothel who thought that the healer costume was a turn-on for his benefit. The wounds from the weapon don't heal, so I use it sparingly."

"You drew blood on Miska."

"And if she apologizes to me, I will allow the wound to heal."

"What if she doesn't? She can be headstrong."

"If she doesn't, she will continue to have a slow line dripping blood until she returns to ask for forgiveness."

He stroked her back slowly. "Let's hope that she does."

They remained in silence for a few minutes and then destroyed the food he had brought in. They had a lot to do for their first day and the first day was just reaching noon.

"These are really good. I normally have to fry an egg and make a sandwich in between clients. This is lovely." She used her right hand only and completed her half of the spread.

They were going to face the afternoon on full stomachs. The demon queen did not like getting the munchies.

Chapter Five

The embarrassment of being in Harrow's arms was nothing compared to being measured and assessed by the seamstress. Tyda was with her and being measured the same way. It was a bit of common nudity that Emrie didn't like but was glad she had a buddy for.

"The harem had simple needs. What are you looking for to lure your demon lord?"

Emrie rapped out her requirements, and the woman widened her eyes and took notes.

"I will also need a very washable outfit for house calls. Folks are not fussy who they bleed on." She smiled tightly.

The seamstress kept her head down and sketched. "What colours are you looking for?"

Emrie smiled. "Dark bronze. I wish to honour my lord in clothing if nothing else. Tyda will be wearing amber with gold trim."

The seamstress's head came up. "She is not wearing the colours of the lord's house?"

Emrie pressed her lips together in a small smirk. "She is wearing the colours of my house. Eventually, our households and staff will be blended, but for now, she and she alone is under my protection. The men will have to fend for themselves."

The seamstress blinked slowly. "I see. So, my lady gets the bill?"

"No, the bills are sent to Reemor, just as they always are, Lilidara." Harrow walked in as if he owned the building.

Emrie ran her hands through her hair

and provided herself with a light cloak for modesty. There were benefits to having locks that felt like silk and acted like steel.

Tyda was wearing a light robe for the fitting, but she squeaked when Harrow entered the room.

Harrow ignored her and walked up to Emrie. "You are very fast with that. I only caught a glimpse of glory."

She wrinkled her nose. "You were trying to glimpse a little too earnestly. Is there something I can do for you?"

His eyelids drooped, and he ran one finger down her torso. "Ah, so many things, but I am simply here to tell you that we have need of your services."

She cocked her head. "What?"

"There is a dignitary who is travelling with his wife. He has suffered an injury, and his wife has gone into labour carrying him back to the stronghold."

His words let her know that she was

dealing with non-humans. That was fine, they would not be her first. "I will just get dressed and attend to them. Where did my supplies end up?"

He smiled and stepped closer. "Your equipment is in the rooms previously occupied by the harem. It has been unpacked for you with the greatest care. Your patients are waiting for you in the outer chamber."

She grinned, grabbed his horns, and pulled him in for a kiss. She could feel the outline of his musculature through his clothing and her hair. The urge to continue, no matter those viewing, was so extreme that she pushed herself away. He was holding her tightly, so it took some doing.

She pushed him back by his horns. "Down, boy. Now, where are my clothes?"

The seamstress snorted. "I burned them. I have had my assistant run this up while we talked."

The long tunic was cut deeply in front and left the curves of her breasts on display. The sleeves were split, so as she raised her hands, her forearms were clear. The open sides from the mid-hip down gave her plenty of space to move.

Lilidara scowled. "And since you insisted, here is the skirt that goes under it."

Emrie shimmied into the full skirt and tied it around her waist before she smoothed the tunic back into place. Once that was done, she pulled her hair out and worked it quickly into a thick braid.

Harrow had taken a seat, and he sighed. "Aw, you put all my toys away."

She chuckled. "They are just away, not gone, and if you refer to me as a toy again, I will turn you from demon lord to eunuch." Her smile was benign and pleasant.

He sat straight. "Can you do that?"

She walked up to him and ruffled his hair. "Push me and find out."

Tyda had scrambled into her clothing while Harrow's attention was fixed elsewhere. "I will take you to the chambers, my lady."

Harrow stood. "I can take her."

Emrie gave him a bland look. "If they haven't removed any trace of your coupling with another woman in those chambers, you had better not be within my sight when I scent it."

He paled. "Ah, right. I will have the cleaners sweep through it a few dozen times."

She nodded and looked to Tyda, winking, before turning back. "Make sure that they do the window ledges and seats as well. As well as every flat surface."

He went from pale to a rich crimson. "I will remain elsewhere."

"You are as wise as you are handsome." She inclined her head to the seamstress. "Thank you, Lilidara."

Lilidara bowed. "I did not think that your ideas would work, but seeing them in place, I now understand. I will have my entire shop working on your order."

"Thank you, but please, excuse me, I believe I have a patient or two. Tyda?"

Tyda nodded and led the way out of the new queen's quarters and through several corridors to the harem. At least they weren't next to Harrow's quarters. That would have irritated her.

Ogres. The couple was ogres. Emrie bustled in, and she took in the lacerations on the face of the male and the puddle on the floor beneath the female.

"Hello, I am Healer Emrie, mage and demon queen. I believe that we should get you both comfortable. Lady, will you help me get your mate into a chair?

Then, we can settle you in once I have stitched his face back together."

The ogress grinned, exposing terrifying teeth. "You know."

"Of course. I have worked with ogres before. You went into labour and struck him, as is your right. It looks like you had something in your hand at the time, so instead of the normal claw imprints, you sliced to the bone."

"My hairpin. I was doing my hair." The woman levered herself to her feet, and together, they managed to get the ogre into the adjoining chamber, which had been arranged as a surgery for Emrie.

"Well, he does move quick."

"My husband?"

Emrie chuckled. "No, mine. He just managed to find me this morning, and the world is conspiring against our mating, but I think he thinks I need some tradition."

The male grunted. "Some women like that."

The female stroked his spiky black hair. "I do like it, Yosh, just not when there is a vise in my belly."

The ogre was set in a chair while his lady squatted next to it. Emrie quickly found the arranged medicines and got some gauze arranged so that she could clean the wound. Her curved needle and thread had been rinsed in spirits and were drying. "Now, if you bite me, I will rip out your tongue and feed it to your newborn."

He blinked at her with shocked black eyes. "I would never bite the demon—ahhh!"

She pressed the cloth to get the caked black blood off and whispered a pain-relief spell while she was at it. He had to feel the pain, or he wouldn't accept that it had stopped.

When she finished with the basic

scouring, she examined the wound. "Just a moment."

She got some pincers and returned. He was rather wary when she reached into the wound over his cheekbone, but as she eased three inches of the pin out of his flesh, he sighed in relief. "I thought there was something."

His voice was gravel over rock.

"Yes, now, I just need to sew the muscle together and then the skin."

"What about Min?"

"She has two hours of hard labour to go before her plate will slide back. I have time to deal with you first."

She pressed him into the chair with one hand on his shoulder, threaded the needle, and started to sew. Tyda was remaining at a safe distance.

"Mistress, do you need me?"

A quick glance up from her work told her the Tyda didn't do well with the surgery. "Can you find someone in Harrow's ranks who is a good medic? I will need an assistant."

Tyda bowed and sprinted out of the room.

Yosh chuckled. "I don't remember ever being that young."

She threaded her needle again. "Neither do I, but I do remember my first time next to someone getting stitches. The scents of blood, fear, sweat, and violence stick with you. It can be hard for humans to get used to."

"Not for you?"

She pulled the needle through his grey skin. "I have never been human, and that is something that most humans have a problem with."

Yosh started to nod and then held his head still as she swiftly closed the wound.

"You will heal well, so I will leave it open to the air until your child is in your arms, though it might be chewing on

67

one of them."

He laughed cautiously and watched as she went over to his wife.

Raising a labouring ogress to her feet took some effort, but after Emrie snapped her with two fingers between the eyes, Min came out of her pain-induced stupor and snapped at Emrie's hand.

"Great. Now that I have your attention, get up, remove your clothing, and get on the table. I will examine you and work at lowering the pain level." Taking the pain entirely away would be inappropriate. The ogres judged their children by how much pain they caused.

Yosh helped Min disrobe, and when she was settled on the table, Emrie covered her with a clean sheet.

A knock at the door made Yosh whirl with a snarl. Emrie let out a light hiss and asked, "Who is it?"

"Private Jamis. I am here to assist

you, my lady."

She looked to Yosh. "Invite him in and have him wash his hands. I will begin the exam. Min, hold still, I am going to check the plate."

An ogress's birth plate slid down from the abdomen to lock the child in the womb. When the child was ready to be born, the plate returned to its position for protecting the internal organs in battle.

Min's birth plate was nearly completely retracted. The feet of the little one were already on their way through the opening.

Jamis came to her side. "What do you need me to do?"

"Have you attended births before?"

"Yes, my lady. My mother is a midwife."

"Good. I want you to get warm water, receiving cloths, a clean robe for the mother, hammer, chisel, and the cleanest, sharpest shears you can find. You have ten minutes."

"I already have the warm water, so I will do the rest in five."

She didn't see him leave, but he was back when she let Min feel all her pain and she started pulling the child free.

The bone plate stopped retracting too early, and the chisel came in handy to chip the half inch of it off in order to pull the little girl free.

Yosh was holding Min's hands and looking at the child. "Is she scarred?"

Emrie took her thumbnail and cut three radiating lines in the girl's forehead. She bit her thumb and rubbed the blood into the cuts.

"Yes, she has been marked by the birth." Emrie handed the pale grey and squalling baby over to her father.

He smiled gratefully. "Thank the gods. Min, Min, our daughter is scarred."

Min looked at him with bleary eyes and then down at her daughter. "She's perfect."

It was then that Emrie realized that Min had no facial scars. It was a sign of triumphant struggle to have facial scars at birth.

"Min, you were born on the day your mother died?"

Min nodded, and Yosh helped her sit up.

A quick peek told Emrie what she needed to know. Min was healing fine, her body was absorbing all traces of the birth and restoring itself to fighting form.

The little one was waving her fists and demanding her first meal. Yosh steered, and Min winced as the little one clamped down.

Emrie straightened from her crouch and took the soiled linens to a basket on the floor. The assistant that she had sent for was busying himself arranging the shelves.

"Jamis?"

"Yes, my lady."

"Well done. You got what was required and didn't panic when confronted with the unusual." She washed her hands in the basin of clean water.

"Thank you, my lady, but all I did was run some errands."

She looked at him and burst out laughing. One night earlier, he had been demanding to see her features, and now, he was threading every curved needle she had and folding them in clean linen.

"You brought me everything that was necessary."

"What were the shears for?"

Emrie glanced over her shoulder at the family that was grunting and snuffling together, their lower teeth jutting out happily.

"The shears were in case the plate

didn't retract. I would have had to go in above it, and that is more than an average blade can stand. The fibres of her womb are like taut bowstrings, they have to be clipped to allow passage."

"Wouldn't that render her unable to conceive?"

"Yes, but if she lived, she would have one child who was healthy and strong."

He leaned in close. "Why did you mark the babe?"

"It is a sign of the fight to be born that every ogre baby experiences. It is also why they adopt or steal humans at every opportunity. A human woman can bear four ogre children before she loses all energy to her offspring. Anyway, the scarring of the face, like the one Yosh has on his left side, is an automatic elevation in rank. He must have been strong to wed Min."

"Because she isn't marked."

"Precisely."

Dawning understanding crossed his face as he looked at the couple, and then, he turned his gaze back to Emrie. "My lady, I am at your beck and call for all your medical emergencies. It seems I have a lot to learn."

She chuckled. "That is the first step. Never fight the knowledge as it comes in. I will ask Harrow to assign you to my service."

He bowed low. "Thank you, my lady."

Harrow entered the space, and his nose wrinkled. Ogress in agony gave off a pheromone that smothered anything a human could produce.

"Lord Yosh, Lady Min, congratulations. Are you able to continue your recuperation in your quarters?" Harrow asked politely.

"Yes, Lord Harrow. I will carry them there, and if you could arrange a meal to be sent to us, we will all recover together."

Harrow inclined his head. "I have already ordered it. Congratulations on your daughter and her splendid markings."

"Thank you for having such a talented mate. She knows what she is doing."

Harrow looked at her, and she knew that she looked horrific. He slowly smiled. "She has talents I haven't even delved into yet."

She licked her lips and smiled in return. The sooner the *delving* could commence, the happier she would be.

Chapter Six

" I will take you back to your quarters so we can have dinner." Harrow offered her his arm.

She stepped toward him and wrapped her hand around his wrist. "Lead the way. I am lost in this place."

He smiled. "I am sure that you will get the hang of it."

Emrie nodded. "Eventually. Directions are my true failing."

He glanced down at her. "I doubt that you have a failing."

"Oh, I have many. You just have to look closely."

He sighed. "I was attempting flattery."

"I know. I am just a little fatigued from staring into the birth canal of an ogress for the last hour."

Harrow winced. "That is killing the mood."

She chuckled. "Apologies, but it is an occupational hazard. Why didn't you call one of the healers from the academy?"

"You are here, and you expressed an interest in continuing your work."

"True."

He walked with her up the steps and in a direction she was unfamiliar with. "Where are we going?"

"I thought you had a bad sense of direction?" He smiled.

"I do, but I can smell water. Is the ogre scent that bad?"

"I would not call it a deal breaker, but yes."

She laughed. "Take me to my bath then, my lord. If you behave, I might let you wash my back."

"I rarely behave."

"I rarely let anyone behind my back." Emrie chuckled.

"You are bizarrely at ease for someone that I want to fuck raw."

She was startled into laughter. "You are not telling me something I didn't know. I have been warned about your sexual appetites for the last decade."

He blinked. "You have?"

"The humans think that to fall into your clutches is the worst, most degrading fate imaginable." She fought her wide grin. "I, however, have a different view of the situation."

They walked into the baths, and when the occupants noticed them, they left immediately. In less than a minute, the pools were empty.

She left her mate and walked to the edge of one pool, gathering some drying sheets before removing her clothing.

Harrow cleared his throat. "What is

The characters and events in this book are fictitious. Any similarity to real persons, living or dead, is coincidental and not intended by the author.

Bride of the Demon King
Copyright © 2019 by Viola Grace
ISBN: 978-1-987969-58-0

©Cover art by Angela Waters

All rights reserved. With the exception of review, the reproduction or utilization of this work in whole or in part in any form by electronic, mechanical or other means, now known or hereafter invented, is forbidden without the express permission of the publisher.

Published by Viola Grace

Look for me online at violagrace.com, Sea to Sky Books, Amazon, Smashwords, Kobo, B&N, and other eBook sellers.

your view?"

She loosened the skirt and let it drop to the ground. "Well, I am the demon queen, but I have no property without my lord. I need him because no one else can give me what I need."

She lifted the tunic and left it on top of the skirt. "So, the exchange will be balanced on both sides. When I take you inside me, we both get what we need."

Emrie looked at him with a challenging expression. "So, are you going to wash my back?"

She wandered over to the shower and rinsed herself from head to toe. When she turned to look at him, he was naked under the shower to her right, and he slowly turned to face her.

"Our destiny is not romantic or the stuff of legends, but we have found each other against considerable odds, and we will guard our people and bring an era of prosperity and health to our lands." He stepped forward and bent his head toward her. "It starts here."

She met his kiss and greeted his tongue with her own. She leaned back in his arms and looked him up and down. "Huh, so your horns aren't the only thing that has grown since I arrived."

He grinned and lifted her in his arms. "All attributed to you, my Queen."

He took a few long strides and stepped into a pool that was so deep, his wings were completely immersed. He held her above the water, and it was a lovely gesture until he dropped her.

She splashed into the water and held her breath while she tried to appear calm. Her heart was pounding, and she struggled to get to the surface again, but it looked so far away.

Emrie burst upward and gasped, moving quickly to the side of the pool.

"Emrie? Emrie?"

She was shaking uncontrollably. With

deliberate motions, she tried over and over to get out of the water, but her arms wouldn't cooperate. Harrow gripped her shoulders and turned her around. "Emrie!"

She looked at him, and the gold flames in his eyes were banked. He was concerned and confused. "Emrie, what's wrong?"

She blinked slowly and whispered, "I can't swim."

She waited for the laughter. There was always laughter. Her body was just too dense to swim.

His eyes widened, and he pulled her to him. "I am sorry. I didn't know."

She nodded. He had been trying to be playful but struggling for her life had definitely killed the mood.

Emrie held onto him as he lifted her out of the pool, heaved himself out, and pulled her onto his lap once again.

The moment that she could feel his

skin under hers, her galloping pulse calmed into a less frenzied beat.

She leaned her head against him, and she chuckled. "So, now you know my weakness."

"It isn't a weakness, it is as much a part of you as your eyes."

He stroked his hand over her hip in a soothing caress.

They remained there while she returned to her snarky self, and his senses must have let him know when it was permissible for him to change his approach.

"Since I have you here, I plan on doing a bit of exploring." His horns glinted in the misty lights of the baths.

"I think that it might be a little awkward to try and do anything in here." Her stomach growled.

Harrow grinned. "It is comforting to know that you have a good appetite."

She blushed slightly and hid her face

against his chest. "Not funny."

"No, it is definitely not funny, but I am still amused. Come on, let's satisfy your hunger."

He stood up, and fire ran from the top of his horns and across both their bodies. She was surprised. She knew she had cleansing fire but had no idea that he did as well.

"As your clothing still smells mightily of ogress, I believe that we should take the private entrance to your quarters."

"There is a private entrance?"

He chuckled. "I designed this stronghold to be a warren of pathways known only to me. There is a door out of every room."

She watched carefully as he walked deeper into the baths and pressed his hand to the wall. There was a click, and the wall slid open, exposing a stairway beyond.

Harrow entered, and the tunnel was

barely big enough for his shoulders and wings.

She smiled. "Let me guess, you designed it when you were shorter?"

He nodded. "About six inches shorter. How did you know?"

"This just seems a little snug for a design. How large do demon kings get in this region?"

He shrugged. "This demesne hasn't had one for three hundred years. The portraits don't have any scale to them."

She giggled. "Did you have your portrait painted?"

"Twice. Once when my wings sprouted and again when the horns arched." He chuckled. "I believe we should have our couple's portrait painted."

She chuckled. "Can I put clothing on first?"

He sighed. "If you wish. I am also going to commission one for our private quarters without clothing."

Emrie laughed. "I doubt you would be able to stand still for the amount of time it takes."

Harrow walked toward a wall and pressed his toes into the groove. Light spilled into the hall, making Emrie aware that they had been moving through darkness. She hadn't noticed, she could see him as clear as day in the hall.

"Wait, did you say *our* quarters?"

"Yes, I was wondering if you were going to insist on a ceremony, but I have decided that you will move to my chambers the moment that the renovations have been completed. In the meantime, I will be staying with you."

She blinked. "What?"

"Clothing and necessities for the next few days have been sent to your quarters." He stepped through the portal, and it closed behind them.

Tyda jumped up as they walked into

the dressing room. "My lord, lady. I did not hear you come in."

Harrow nodded to her. "Has the meal been prepared?"

"It is waiting in the bedchamber." Tyda kept her gaze down.

"Good. You are dismissed for the evening." Harrow gave the order.

Tyda looked up in surprise. "Mistress?"

"Go to your sleeping quarters for the night. I will see you in the morning." Emrie looked up at Harrow. "I can walk, you know."

He grinned, his gold eyes sparkling. "I know, but it is my pleasure to keep you in my arms."

Tyda watched their playful banter for a moment, and then, she left the room with a bewildered smile, shaking her head.

The bedchamber was sparsely decorated, which suited Emrie just fine.

There was a table set up in the corner with covered dishes on it and one chair.

"I don't think that is an invitation to company." She chuckled.

"I think that it is exactly what it is."

As they got closer, she saw the peculiar structure of the chair. The back was a narrow spine reinforced with steel. "Oh, so I am the one with a missing chair."

"As long as I am with you, you will always have a place." Still naked, Harrow settled into his chair and helped her to sit up straight.

His erection had not diminished in the slightest, and she had to mutter, "If your cock continues in that condition for another few hours, you are going to have to consult a healer."

He whispered in her ear as he leaned forward to uncover the dishes. "I know just where to find one."

Chapter Seven

It started with something small. She was eating one of the desserts, and some cream escaped its confines and landed on her breast. Harrow tidied it up with his tongue, and then, she was being used to push the dishes aside.

Emrie tried to touch him, but he was everywhere at once. The moist sound and feel of his mouth set her on fire. When he dragged his tongue over her breasts, she could feel the blaze of heat left behind. It felt like live flames were following in his wake.

She whimpered as she fought to memorize the sensations. The wet heat that she had produced earlier was slick-ing her thighs. Harrow sniffed and then inhaled deeply before he pried her thighs apart and burrowed into her sex with mindless enthusiasm.

She yelped and then gasped when he delved into her with his tongue. With nothing else to hang onto, she gripped his horns and used them to steer him to the places that sent sparks through her soul.

Emrie could feel the smile against her, the devilishly sharp teeth were in evidence, but he nipped, lapped, and sucked until release caused her body to buck wildly.

She heard the hoarse screams and felt fire rip through her. By the time her body had stopped thrashing, he was over her and his cock pressed against her.

He winked. "Keep a grip on the horns."

She looked up, and her hands were hanging onto him while he held her hips, and ever so slowly, he moved into her.

His back was arched, and he leaned in to kiss her as he completed their joining.

She stroked the side of his face and ran her fingers through his hair as his hips began to slide against hers. The delightful friction led to a swift rise in pleasure once again, and she screamed into his mouth, but he simply continued until the pulse was building again.

If she had been human, this probably would have hurt, but fortunately, she was not.

Their kiss involved a lot of biting and some snarling by the time her third release was thundering through her. He locked in place and began to buck and shudder as he held tight to her.

"So, why didn't you tell me that I had my own small bath?" She leaned back on the edge of the tub.

Harrow was wearing a towel, and his hair was damp from his shower. "I didn't tell you, because I can't fit into this one. I had been looking forward to a slick and naked you in my arms."

Emrie chuckled and wrinkled her nose. "I just wish that gravy hadn't been involved."

He grinned. "It made for fun cleanup, and I got you to scrub my back. Getting in between the wings can be tricky."

She snorted and touched her damp hair. "Are you sure that we got it all out of my hair?"

"I am sure." He sighed. "I have never enjoyed brushing a woman's hair more than yours, my Queen."

Emrie wrinkled her nose. "You did not have to check for tangles with your wings."

"I did. It is the best way." The innocent expression was somewhat hampered by the horns.

She chuckled and yawned.

"I suppose that this excellent start to our first day together has come to an end. Come on, I will dry you."

Emrie put her hands on the edges of the tub and heaved herself to standing. He wrapped her in a cloth and set her on another one before kneeling and drying her gold skin from head to toe.

She snickered as he picked her up and carried her to the bed that was barely large enough for him. He curled her against his body, and he whispered, "I am very happy to accept my tribute."

He laughed outright when she elbowed him in the ribs before trying to settle in a bed occupied by another living being. She could sleep on lumpy benches, in chairs, and leaning against walls, but it was odd to have a person in contact with her.

She inhaled deeply and matched her breathing to his. It was a very successful day as the demon's bride. Emrie looked forward to the next.

She woke to feel something nibbling at her ear. She gasped and moved away. For some reason, the tip of her ear was extremely sensitive.

Harrow chuckled, and his voice was husky when he said, "Good morning, my Queen."

She rolled over and rubbed the tip of the ear he had been nibbling. It was not the same shape it had been before. "What the hells?"

She flipped the bedding off and walked across the chamber with long strides. In her dressing room, she looked in the mirror and blinked several times before she realized intellectually that it was her own reflection.

"What..."

Her ears were pointed and rose high to a sharp peak that her hair couldn't cover. Her skin was a darker shade of gold, and her eyes looked like they were pools of ruby flame. The truly disturbing thing was that her hair was writhing softly, shifting and coiling before hanging straight.

Harrow followed her, and he wrapped his arms around her. "Your beauty is beyond compare, Emrie."

She looked up at him and opened her mouth, seeing sharp fangs on her upper and lower jaw. "I feel a little different this morning."

He chuckled. "You are complete now. I have felt my own changes, but I will test them later."

She wasn't in a position to look and see if he had two penises, but she could wait for later to ascertain that he hadn't picked up that rare adaptation. Right now, she was concerned that she hadn't known about the changes.

"Was this in your books? It wasn't in

94

mine."

He was slowly moving his hands over her, relearning her after the changes.

She paused. "Wait, am I taller?"

"A few inches."

"Damn. Lilidara is going to be furious."

He chuckled and leaned in to kiss her neck. "She will adapt. She used to work for my mother and came here when I set up my own household."

Emrie sighed and tilted her head to one side. He smiled at her in the mirror and continued to work his lips and tongue over the column of her neck. When his hand slid between her thighs, she took a slight step to one side, inviting him in.

He cupped her breasts in turn while his fingers drove her to distraction.

Watching the colouration of her skin darken and light move where he touched was an eye-opening experience. If she focused, she could see flames under his hands. He smiled when she started to make those small noises that he delighted in.

By the time she was on the brink, he was sliding two fingers in and out of her while her inner muscles gripped him tightly. When her release struck, he held her tightly as she rode his hand, his thumb pressing on the small nub of flesh that was the centre of the storm.

She slumped in his arms.

He chuckled. "This is the image that I want to hang in our quarters. You satisfied in my arms."

She smiled slowly and was turning to him, reaching to return the favour when there was a knock at the door to the outer chamber.

A feminine throat cleared, and Tyda said, "My lord, there is an urgent matter that Reemor wishes to discuss with you."

Emrie chuckled. "The timing is unfortunate, my lord, but your responsibilities are heavy and must be attended to." She ran her hand up and down his cock slowly before trailing it away.

He grunted and gave her a narrow-eyed look. "They will, and then, I will attend to you, my whimsical Queen."

He patted her butt before he turned away and went to the wardrobe.

His clothing choice was a knee-length skirt and boots. Nothing else was necessary.

"I am guessing that I should get dressed as well for breakfast if nothing else."

He went to her dressing table and found a brush. With quick strokes, he got his locks in order.

"I will be in my office unless someone tells you otherwise. If things change, I will send a messenger."

She nodded and went to her wardrobe. She slid on some thigh-high boots and grabbed a tunic that wrapped in a deep vee and was open to the hip. The sash that hung with it wrapped around her and uplifted her breasts a fairly obscene amount.

"Harrow, before you go, can I have Private Jamis?"

He had been watching her dress, and he jerked his head so that he was now looking at her face.

She smiled and pulled her hair down, braiding it in loops that set off her ears. "Private Jamis, I would like him for my private household. He is a prime candidate to be my apprentice."

"You can have six chosen men in your private guard and as many ladies' maids as you wish. I will order Reemor to prepare lodgings for your private corp."

He was in front of her in an instant, holding her head and kissing her until her mouth was aching and swollen, as were other parts of her.

Before she could grab him and haul him back to bed, he was gone.

"Damn, he moves fast for such a big guy."

She grinned and went to the dressing table mirror to finish arranging her hair.

Tyda came in and looked at her in surprise. "My lady. You look... different."

"I am aware of it. It is apparently a side effect of our union." She grinned. "He got taller, too. He doesn't fit his trousers anymore. It is skirts for him until he can get some new ones made up."

Tyda blinked. "Is that common? I mean, will I change like that?"

Emrie looked at her little demoness. "Eventually. You will need a demon lord to trigger the final changes, but learning and putting what you learn into action is what will drive your own transformation. I am a little sorry to have burdened you with it. I was rather focused on the moment."

"So, I will have to marry a demon lord?"

Emrie rocked one hand from side to side. "Marry is a loose term. You will have to mate with one to gain your full power."

"Aren't I too old for that?"

Emrie stood up, and Tyda stared up at her.

"No, Tyda, you are not too old to let yourself learn and grow. It is a parasitic situation that has caused the demon lord tradition of taking brides that have just reached adulthood. The males are afraid of being controlled by the females simply because if we have the right education, we are infinitely stronger and can do things they could never dream of."

Tyda whispered, "Like to make demons?"

Emrie grinned and went to her, giving her a careful hug. "That is only one of the things that you can do, and I wouldn't recommend it until you are somewhere secure and have the skills and strength to defend your new demon."

"Defend?"

"Yes, every single demon lord who is looking for a match is going to be knocking on our doorstep."

Tyda looked nervous. "Why?"

"Because brides can die. They can be raised in confinement and weak. If they don't have an opportunity to be strong, they won't be. Those brides can elevate their demon lord slightly, but they soon die."

Tyda blinked. "Why?"

"Find me a place to eat, and I can discuss this further. Oh, and if you have a chance, have Jamis found. I am going to make him an offer, and you, you are not going to be traded like a farm animal ever again. When you choose your mate, it will be your choice, and he will be lucky to have you."

"Yes, my lady." Tyda smiled shyly.

They left the queen's chamber and down toward the hall workmen were bustling and shouting orders to each other. It seemed that the king's chamber was actually being given an overhaul.

Tyda led her past the men, and Emrie heard the clattering of tools as she approached. Her tunic was full enough below the waist to keep her covered if she was standing still, but walking, her boots and the skin of her upper thighs would flash with every step. The cleavage on display was more than she had ever shown in her lifetime, but today, it felt appropriate.

The men bowed low, and some knelt on the ground as she passed. When they were out of earshot, she murmured to Tyda, "I didn't think my hair was that good today."

Tyda laughed. "I think it is your presence and your added height, my lady."

"Ah. Yes. Things do have a slightly different perspective. So, where are we finding breakfast?"

"The great hall, my lady. The kitchen staff will serve us there, and you can meet some of your people or, at least, be on display to them."

"Ah, yes. That part of things. I wonder if the ogres are still here."

"They are. They have plans to leave later in the day after they get you to bless their daughter with a name."

"Bless? Oh my. That is going to take a bit of thought."

"Have you done it before, my lady?"

"Twice but not an ogre child. I am not quite sure what to bless them with."

Tyda gave her a small smile. "I am sure you will think of something."

"So, when do you think Lilidara will have your clothing ready?"

"Aside from this gown, she has delivered two different dresses. Your colours will be in action tomorrow." Tyda smiled. "Thank you again for accepting me. I did not want to be dismissed to another demon lord habitat."

"The others?"

"They scattered, grabbed their jewels and headed out the moment they were able. It means that the stronghold is short a few dozen men, but no one in their right mind would attack a newly mated demon lord."

Emrie snorted. "Except another demon lord would consider it a moment of weakness. Either way, I will feel better after a meal."

"Right this way, my demon Queen."

They were still giggling softly as they entered the hall and all conversation stopped. It seemed that some of the occupants were appalled that their lord had managed to find his match, but some of them might have wanted her to be shorter. Finding a bench to fit would be tricky, but fortunately, she had a new assistant to show her the way.

Chapter Eight

Seated a few feet from the throne was a peculiar place to have breakfast, but everyone in the kitchen brought her their breakfast specialties and introduced themselves. It was a nice, casual court. Emrie liked it.

Tyda watched quietly and politely as the kitchen staff presented their best. It was when they had returned to the kitchen that Emrie pulled the faces for some of the food combinations.

She was nearly finished with her tea when Harrow came striding in through the main doors. *Damn.* He really did leave the building in the skirt.

She sipped at her tea while he approached, and he inclined his head. "My Queen, we are about to have visitors. Are you ready for your debut?"

She got a few bits of information from that sentence. It was another demon lord, he was coming armed, and he didn't yet have a bride.

She smiled calmly. "Tyda, please go to my medical chamber and alphabetize the books for two hours or until I call."

Harrow looked relieved. Emrie finished her tea and got to her feet, standing next to him. "Where do you want me? Next to the throne? Left, right?"

"On the throne. It is yours, after all. Feir will choke when he sees you."

She walked with him to the throne room while a cloud of servants scrubbed everything in a wave that left the room smelling of lemon and mint.

The retainers on hand gasped as he took her hand and settled her in the throne. She was glad she had worn boots. She would be terrifying enough as it was without her arched feet making her tunic slip and exposing way too much thigh.

Tyda disappeared in the stronghold, and Emrie heaved a sigh of relief. There were a few things she wanted to do today and fighting a strange demon lord wasn't one of them.

Emrie shifted slightly and placed her hands on the arms of the seat. She grimaced. If she had thought about things instead of acting, she wouldn't have transformed Tyda quite so soon. It had felt like the right choice, but she had been a little freaked out at being the only female in the interior of the stronghold. She had literally made a friend.

Harrow stood next to her with his wings flexed wide. His men arranged themselves in even lines, and Reemor stood at the base of the dais.

At the end of the hall, the doors

opened, and a demon lord strode in with his men stomping in behind him.

Emrie scowled. That was going to be a lot of mud for the housekeepers to scrub away. *How rude.*

The demon lord swanned up and stood with his legs apart, leering at her. "So, this is the little bitch?"

Reemor cleared his throat. "Presenting Demon Lord Feir."

Emrie smirked. "Ah, a chosen name."

The lord flared his wings out. "What?"

"You chose your name. How ridiculous. Let me see what your name was." She got up and let her impulse carry her to the edge of the dais. His head was even with her breasts, but that didn't matter. He was too stunned to do anything.

"Ah, there it is. Dorwin. Your birth name was Dorwin." She stared into his eyes and saw his entire childhood and

109

his developing cruelty. When she got to his treatment of his women, she curled her lip. "You are definitely more suited to the name you were born with."

She turned her back and headed back for the throne. She felt the heat of his hand as he reached out to grab her, and Harrow's wing snapped the side of his arm, slicing it wide.

Emrie returned to the throne. "So, you have come here to Harrow's home for what reason?"

Feir was holding his arm to stop the bleeding. "Damn you. She should get what is coming to her."

Harrow inclined his head. "I do agree. Please answer my Queen. Why have you come here, Feir?"

Feir looked at Harrow and raised his brows. He reached to grab his sword and winced. He had to settle for gesturing to his men. "I have come to take your bride, Harrow. You are far too weak to keep her."

Emrie laughed from the depths of her soul. "That is not happening. Not in this life, nor the next."

Feir smirked as his men stepped forward. "It is happening, little bitch."

"Little? I don't suppose you noticed, but I am at least two inches taller than you. Besides, you and Harrow should handle this. It is what demon lords do, do they not?"

She reached out to Harrow, and when he took her hand, she pressed a kiss to it. She sent him energy and good wishes with that kiss.

"May I fight in your defense?"

She grinned. "Please. I look forward to rewarding you later."

He winked, and he moved to stop the encroaching warriors from making it to the dais.

Emrie watched the strong muscles of his back flex and twist as his wings slashed and speared the men who were rushing them.

The sounds of battle and the scent of blood filled the air. Emrie inhaled deeply and was a little surprised to find that the scent didn't fill her with any sort of agitation. As a healer, the smell of blood was a call to action, but now, she was amused by it.

When one of the attackers made it past Harrow, Emrie simply stood up and looked down at the man with fire in her eyes.

He stopped in his tracks and fell to his knees, his sword out of his hand.

"Forgive me, my lady."

She reached down and stroked his hair. "Look up at me."

He looked at her, and she smiled at him. "Will you swear fealty to me? Remain in my service?"

He blinked. "I am sworn to Lord Feir."

"I can break your oath, but you would be mine to call upon until death."

His smile was instant. "I am yours, my Queen."

She crouched and kissed him, breathing her power into him. "Stand, Doryn, and join my King's ranks."

He stood, looking at his hands as they darkened to a mahogany-bronze. His horns pushed out of his forehead, and his tunic tore as his wings sprouted. She had not been expecting it to happen that quickly. She must have dosed him a little too much.

He stood up and watched his claws grow.

Emrie had to stop watching him as more men poured into the hall. "Really?"

She watched Harrow finally closing with Feir, and she twisted her lips while she fought the urge to help the men who were lying wounded.

She was about to leave the hall to stop the urge to heal all of them when she saw him, Jamis. He was lying on the ground and breathing hard through the wound in his torso. He was hers!

She walked past the warring men and found her healing assistant, looking him in the eyes. "Do you still want to learn the healing arts?"

His eyes were wild, but he nodded.

"Will you devote yourself to me, as my apprentice?"

He nodded, he tried to speak, but a bubble of blood was all that emerged.

Her kiss had a different purpose this time. She needed to heal as well as create a bodyguard. The trickle of energy did what it needed to do, but when her energy coursed through Jamis, the transformation was controlled.

She whispered against his mouth, "I give you speed, cunning, strength, and wisdom. When you are ready, Jamis,

114

you will learn the arts of magic and healing."

His body was arcing with the change. She stood up and clapped her hands.

The fighting around her ceased immediately.

Doryn was at her side, the swords in his hands were dripping blood. She had no idea he was ambidextrous.

Harrow had Feir on the ground. The smaller, older, weaker demon lord was on his back, bleeding from dozens of deep cuts.

"Harrow, I believe that this has been a sufficient demonstration. Are you satisfied?"

He looked at her, his gold eyes flaring. "He dared to try and take you."

"And I would not go. You know how stubborn I am after knowing me only one day."

He let out a laughing huff, and he nodded. "I have noticed. How did you stop the battle?"

"You were all frightened by a loud noise and a sudden snap. And a bit of magic. That is part of being what I am, and why a demon like Feir could never handle a demon queen. This is my house, and I will not tolerate violence, so there will be no violence. Simple."

She walked through the wounded and stood next to Feir. "You don't know what it is to learn to be a man, so I will give you the chance to do it all over."

Emrie was acting on the instincts of her magic, so she crouched and pressed a hand into the bloody mess of Feir's chest.

He screamed as she pulled the essence of demon lord from him and left him as nothing but a lesser demon. She didn't like the taste of his magic, but she needed to process it until it was fit for use again.

He was still screaming when she

stood, so she kicked him. "Get up. I healed your wounds when I demoted you."

Feir looked at her. "You have no power over me."

She shook her head. "No, I have no power over him." She jerked her thumb in Harrow's direction. "A demon in my territory is mine to tear apart at will. You have strayed into my home, and you were not invited. If you behave and work for what you get, you will become a demon lord again in ten years. A lesser one but still a demon lord. If you find a strong queen to take you on, you might even rise to king, but abuse women on the way and the queen will stay out of your path. I will see to it. Oh, and your name is now Lesser Demon Dorf."

He was hissing so much he was foaming at the mouth. "What power do you have?"

"I have the power of a demon queen,

the first true queen in over three hundred years. I can make demons, and I can destroy demons. I also make an excellent lemon squash."

She walked over to Harrow, and in front of those assembled, she went on her knees. "My lord, my husband, my king. You are mine as I am yours. The one man I will bow to, and the only man I will listen to. To you, I pledge myself in front of these witnesses."

Instead of lifting her, he knelt with her in the blood and mud. "My bride, my wife, my queen. I am yours as you are mine. You are the one woman I will bow to, and I will always listen to you. To you, I pledge myself, my home, my power, and my honour in front of these witnesses."

Their kiss sealed their pledge, and she was smiling at him as a little more power rippled through him. She had no idea where that energy was going, but she knew it was going to end up somewhere fun.

Chapter Nine

When Feir's... Dorf's men had left, there was nothing left for Harrow and his men to do but clean up.

She had the very wounded men carried to the new surgery while Jamis and Doryn helped her gather the supplies she would need.

The beds were arranged in a long line, which was amusing considering the sparse nature of the space the day before, but she liked it. She triaged the injuries and went to work. Part of her brain identified men who would make excellent lesser demons as she stitched, wrapped, pressed, and treated each of the dozen injured men.

Jamis and Doryn did their jobs admirably. They lifted and carried for her with lovely dexterity, and Jamis's skill at making pain potions could not be ignored.

She felt a sense of satisfaction when all the men had been tended to and were on the mend. A few trickles of magic had been let loose to pull some away from the precipice of death, but she had not made any more demons.

Emrie washed her hands and felt Harrow enter the infirmary. "Has Dorf and his men been seen on their way?"

Harrow chuckled. "Yes. I cannot believe you renamed him."

"I also sent a spell along with him. His men will only call him Lord Dorf now." Her smile was smug. She tried to make it aloof, but it wasn't going to happen.

"I do not know how long he will be in power." Harrow wrapped her in his arms and rubbed his chin on her hair.

"Oh, because his property can't belong to a lesser demon?"

"Because now he is a jackass with no power."

She snuggled back against him and sighed at the feeling of warmth that flooded through her. "Right. That could be a problem for him."

"What will his people do without a leader?" Harrow asked her softly.

"Have a party?"

"Seriously. They need a demon lord to lead them." He nudged her head with his jaw, and she was soon staring at Doryn.

She blinked until she caught on. "Oh, come on. I just made him!"

"And it was for a purpose. You gave him a lot of power, and as it finishes integrating with his body, he will be stronger than Dorf ever was."

She snickered. The spell was holding.

She watched as Doryn went from bed

to bed, caring for the wounded and making the men laugh. He had a knack for it.

"I would have to ask him. He has fealty to me and is loyal to you. I was hoping to develop him a bit."

"My dearest queen, you had wings ripping out of his back and horns shooting out of his forehead. I think he has had enough development."

She leaned back against him. "Fine. I will ask him."

"Please. The less issue that the folk have and the sooner they can recover from Dorf's reign, the better."

"What will he have to do to Dorf?"

"He will have to kill him."

"Right. Of course. That idiot wouldn't take *fuck off* for an answer." She squeezed the bridge of her nose with a finger and thumb.

She looked up and pasted a bright smile on her face. "Doryn, come here, please."

Doryn looked at her and came right over, bowing low to her and Harrow. "How may I be of service, my Queen?"

"I know today has been a busy day for you, but how would you like to have your own demesne?"

He looked at her and blinked. "My own demesne?"

"Yes, Demon Lord Feir is no more. He is now a lesser demon, and he was not a good master to begin with. I did not think of it, but if I put a weak demon in charge of a people, they will be targets for other demon lords to prey on. I am offering you his home and space." She cleared her throat. "You may have to kill him."

Doryn smiled slowly, his fangs were showing. "I look forward to it. Thank you for this opportunity."

Harrow spoke. "I will send a dozen men with you to back up your claim, but I can feel the demons stirring, so you had best get new armour and get on your steed."

"Can I wear armour with wings?"

Harrow pressed a kiss to Emrie's cheek. "Excuse me, but I need to explain some of the finer points of being a demon to Doryn."

"Of course. Just one thing."

Emrie stepped up to Doryn, and she whispered a spell of protection against his cheek. "Be brave, be safe, be wise."

He smiled at her, and his eyes flared brightly for a moment before his gaze shifted behind her, and it dimmed. "Thank you, my Queen."

"Stop glaring at him, Harrow."

She heard a chuckle and continued her spell work. She wrapped Doryn in everything she could think of to protect him, and she realized she may have gone too far when he darkened to a deep purple. "Oh dear. I think I overprotected you."

Harrow gently pulled her away. "Stop mothering him. He will be fine. I have seen him fight."

Emrie sighed and stepped aside, watching her mate lead her new demon lord away.

She looked over at Jamis, and he held up his hands. "I am fine like this, mistress. I would rather learn the healing arts from you than sprout wings and rule."

She cocked her head. "There must be something you want."

"I want to learn, and I want to do it quickly."

She smiled and reached out for him.

Jamis ducked away from her hand and held his palms up. "Really, mistress. I am fine the way I am."

Emrie pouted. "I really wanted to give you something. I have a lot of extra energy after taking power away from Dorf."

Jamis gave her a wary look. "Fine, mistress, but nothing that alters my mind or changes my physical appearance. Please."

Emrie pursed her lips and thought. "May I give you something that will increase your ability to serve me, as long as it meets the criteria?"

He sighed. "Yes, my lady."

She placed her hands on his shoulders and focused. The energy went into him, and it went dormant in his body. It would be there when he or she needed it.

She pulled her hands back. "There. Thank you."

He narrowed his eyes. "What did you do?"

"I gave you speed. It won't activate unless you will it to. I would recommend you experimenting outside so that you can work at scaling your actions to your speed."

"Are you sure?"

She grinned. "The worst thing that will happen is that you will go for a run in a pasture."

"Fair enough. I will try it later. For now, I need to tend to our patients."

Emrie grinned. "Excellent. Call me if you need me. You merely need to whisper my name, and I will be on my way."

He blinked.

She winked. "New feature. Enjoy."

She walked out of the infirmary and was on her way to the main hall when she caught the scent of ogre and Tyda.

"Yosh, Min, are you going already?" She paused and bowed slightly.

Min grunted and jutted out her lower jaw. "My lady, would you do us the honour of naming our child?"

The baby was thrust at Emrie, and she took it carefully. "Of course. Let's go into the courtyard and do the naming in the light of day."

The ogres grinned, and Tyda nodded.

Emrie led the way through the halls until they passed the dais and ended up in the bright sunlight with the sun sparkling down on them.

She turned and smiled at them with the baby blinking in the bright light.

"Yosh and Min, I don't know what brought you here, but I am delighted that you were here for me. Distracting me on my first day let me know that there would be a place for me here, and while I know that the labour was far from convenient, it helped me a lot."

The ogres inclined their heads but remained quiet.

"Since you have given me this, this place in a new world that I am going to shape around me, I will give your daughter the name Tekka. The goddess who shapes the earth."

Yosh blinked, and then, he grinned wide. "My lady, how did you know we came from a clan of potters? Tekka is ideal."

Emrie held the baby up and gave her a tiny flicker of power. "Tekka, I give you a keen eye and steady hands. You will be a master artisan, and I will defend your right to practice your craft."

She pressed a kiss to the scar on the child's head and leaned back before the baby could land a bite. "Well done, little one. Be well and be strong, Tekka."

She handed the child back to her mother, and the ogres bowed and bowed again, thanking her for the name.

"It is my pleasure. I know that pottery is traditionally male in your clan, but she will take on the challenge. If any of the guilds or clans have an issue with her skill, call on me. I will defend her right to craft her own future."

Emrie could feel Harrow approaching. "Have you concluded your business with Lord Harrow?"

Yosh nodded. "We have constructed a

trade agreement and a path for our merchants to travel."

"Excellent. I didn't want that lost in between the excitement."

Min put little Tekka in a carry sling. "Why is there so much blood about?"

"Ah, there was a territorial dispute. It was settled."

Min blinked. "Which territory?"

Harrow came up to them and put his arm around Emrie's waist. "Demon Queen Emrie."

She blushed. "Something like that. A demon lord thought he could oust Lord Harrow, and he found out he was mistaken."

"He also thought he could claim a grown demon queen, and he will never make that particular mistake again."

She scowled. "Did you make sure of it?"

Harrow nodded. "I did."

She huffed. "I would have liked to

have said goodbye."

"He will be fine. You loaded him up with so much magic you turned him purple. He will be fine." Harrow laughed.

She leaned into him. "Fine, but if my creation gets a hangnail, I am blaming you."

Yosh and Min were looking at them, and slow smiles spread over their features.

Emrie blinked. "Where are my manners? Harrow, you know Yosh and Min. This is baby Tekka."

He inclined his head. "Congratulations on the safe arrival. Do you require an escort to your home?"

Yosh shook his head. "No, we are meeting our trading caravan in a few hours. If all goes well, we will have product to show you when we return to this stronghold."

Min chuckled. "Tekka might be walking by then, but I look forward to seeing you again, Queen Emrie."

"You are welcome, Mother Min." Emrie bowed. "Be kind to your family and care for them as well as they deserve."

The ogres grinned, bowed, and backed away before turning and heading for the stables.

Emrie watched the small tasks of life taking place around her. "Is this really where I live now?"

"It is. Don't worry. It will become less normal when you pay attention." He swung her into his arms and carried her back into the stronghold. Apparently, he was interested in helping to anchor her to her new home.

Chapter Ten

*P*leasure was Harrow's means of distracting her. She had to admit that most of the time it worked.

Emrie was standing on the tallest wall of the stronghold and looking out at the sunrise. Two weeks had come and gone since the night of tribute. She had delivered three babies in the city, lectured once at the healing academy, and set four broken limbs. It wasn't enough.

Emrie drummed her fingers against the wall, and she tried to think of what she could do next.

"You are needed in the great hall, my lady." Tyda appeared out of the shadow like she tended to. It was her mastered skill. She had desired to not be seen, so she wasn't.

"Lovely. I am on my way."

Tyda bowed and backed into the shadows with a grin.

Emrie left her self-absorption to head down to the great hall. Lilidara had begun to embroider the wide-sleeved tunics that Emrie wore, and today, she was wearing dark burgundy with gold thread.

The guards and servants that she passed in the halls bowed with slight smiles on their faces. She had assuaged their fears during that first battle in the great hall. She was on their side, and aside from the cosmetic changes, Jamis was the same man he had been before. That little fact had been a relief for those men who had gone through training with him.

It was funny that Jamis's volunteering to be her assistant had reaped such benefits for her relationships with those in the stronghold. He was enjoying learning about medicine, and it had only recently come about that she learned he had been rejected from the healing academy. He had not been wealthy enough to attend. Now that he had a chance to learn, he wasn't wasting it.

She hummed to herself as she walked through the halls until she entered the archway that led to the great hall. Harrow was standing and speaking with a high-ranking couple. He turned toward her and smiled when she entered the hall.

Emrie kept her posture straight and tried to make her expression friendly.

Harrow held his hand out, and she placed her fingers in his. He pulled her to his side. "Mother, Father, this is my bride, Emrie, Demon Queen."

He turned to Emrie. "Emrie, this is my father, Lord Algus Twell, and his wife, Lady Murian Twell. They have come to meet you."

Emrie smiled at the couple, and they were staring at her in shock. "I am pleased to meet you both. You raised a fine son."

Her words seemed to break some sort of trance.

Lord Twell cleared his throat. "Thank you. He was always focused on his mission, and it made him the man he is."

Emrie looked at her mate and then back to his parents. "His mission?"

Lady Twell smiled. "You, dear. From the moment you were born, he was aware of you, and he did what he could to make himself into the kind of man you would want. We did what we could to help him, but he knew what he wanted to achieve."

Emrie blinked and felt a blush start on her cheeks. "I see. I... don't know what to say to that."

Harrow chuckled. "I did tell you that this was all for you."

"Yes, but you didn't say that your mother knew."

Lord Twell smiled. "I greet you warmly, daughter."

He held out his hands, and she placed her hands over his. He was a small man, and she had to lean down considerably to get the kiss on each cheek that he offered.

"You are a well-formed, lass." His eyes were twinkling.

"It comes with the skin colour. I was a scrawny child." She tried to release his hands, but it was his wife clearing her throat that got his attention enough to let her go.

"She doesn't want to hurt you, fool." Lady Twell smiled. "Could you show me the infirmary, daughter?"

"I would be happy to... Lady Twell."

The older woman took Emrie's arm.

"Call me Murian if you can't call me mother."

"Murian then. I have never called anyone mother." She smiled to take the sting out of it.

Murian blinked rapidly, and she cleared her throat. "So, the tour?"

"This way." She led the older woman away from Harrow and his father.

They were just out of earshot and in the corridor past the great hall when Murian began the questions. "Who raised you, child?"

Emrie smiled. "I was raised by a series of folk who thought that another demon lord with a bride would be a disaster. They fed me, clothed me, but it was only the last couple who educated me."

"Hm. How dare they say that about my boy?" Murian was irritated by the thought.

"How did you deal with raising a

demon?"

Murian shrugged. "It took some stern words on my part."

"Harrow was a handful?"

"No, Akin was always a good boy. His father kept goading him to stronger and stronger acts. He gave him weapons, men who were willing to give their loyalty to him. When it came time to seek you out, my husband was waiting for you to come home with our son so that he could spend the next decade telling you that you were a lucky woman."

Emrie laughed. "I have no doubt, but since I was eleven at the time and being spirited away by the same organization who wanted to hide me, he would have had a fight on his hands."

"I am sure that the men with you would have surrendered you."

"Not that. I was never one to follow orders. If he had demanded that I come with him, I would have run, and I would have gotten away." She smiled slightly.

"How can you be so sure?"

"I know myself, and I know that I was not keen on being stuffed in a cage at that time. If I were away from my caregivers, I would have run. I thought about it constantly. I wasn't going to him until I was ready."

Murian had a smile in her voice. "So, you were ready?"

"I was. I am. The magic in me has matured, and I can control it most of the time."

"Is that what happened to my son?"

Ah, so that was where the questions were leading. "I have given your son something he was missing, the catalyst to the next phase of his power. He has gone from demon lord to demon king. It is something that many claim but few achieve."

"What about his other women? Did you destroy them?"

Emrie snorted. "No. Harrow dismissed them. Once he had me, he didn't need them anymore."

"That is rather arrogant."

"It sounds like it, doesn't it? But that is why the gods paired us. We are matched in every way." With every passing day, Emrie was convinced of it.

"I suppose. I always thought that his bride would be petite and need protecting. It was an image in my mind."

They were approaching the infirmary. "Would it make you feel better if you knew I used to be four to six inches shorter than I am now, and I really did need him to care for me? His affection has helped me to grow in every way."

She led her mother-in-law into the infirmary and showed her around. The subject matter suddenly shifted, and Murian pelted her with questions about cleanliness and herbal freshness.

Emrie answered her while the older

woman was watching Jamis help the last of the men injured in the great hall battle walk up and down the aisle between the beds.

"Who is that?"

Emrie had a maternal smile, and she knew it. "Jamis, my apprentice. He has taken to the study of medicine with alacrity. He would have been a master healer if his family had been able to send him to the academy."

"Why didn't they?"

"Like most folk, he was born poor. It has a dramatic effect on your possible education opportunities."

"Is he a young demon? Is Akin fine with this?"

"He is a lesser demon, he is my personal apprentice, Harrow has authorized me to have a total of six of them."

"Men? He has authorized you to have six men?"

"Men, women. I also have an assistant who used to be in his harem. She asked to join my service, so I gave her the tools to do so. She is thriving as well. It is good to see."

"May I speak with Jamis?"

"Of course. I will be here if you have any additional questions."

Emrie turned her back and let Murian ask Jamis about his life before the transformation and his life after. He spoke honestly about being nervous, but his confidence in his abilities was increasing when he watched the men get up and walk out after being healed.

Murian asked if Emrie had ever used her demon wiles on him. Jamis laughed and informed her that while the energy to transform him was delivered with a kiss, there was only power and never lust in her eyes when she came near him. She wanted to give and give. He just didn't know how much he could safely take before he went from lesser demon to demon lord.

The rest of the conversation didn't interest Emrie. She did an inventory to keep track of which herbs they needed to collect and which they needed to purchase. Jamis was taking to herbology with a strange intensity. He had lost a family member to a simple fever, and the loss was now driving his urge to learn. It wasn't the worst reason to seek out an education that Emrie had ever heard. Many folks did it just because they could afford it.

She spoke softly, "Tyda, could you please check with the gardeners to see if these plants are on hand? If not, I will need to take a trip to the market."

She folded the list and held it up between two fingers.

Tyda took the page from her and whispered, "Yes, my lady."

The paper and the demoness disappeared in shadow.

Emrie cocked her head. That was going to take some getting used to, but Tyda had asked for the ability to hide wherever she was. Shadow was the best bet.

Emrie looked out the window at the open meadow, and she focused. If she looked at it in a certain way, she could almost make out a building that had yet to be created. That was foolish, who would build an academy so close to the city.

* * * *

"So, son, you have grown." Lord Twell sat across the table from Harrow.

Harrow laughed. "Yes, yes, I have."

"Did it hurt?"

Harrow closed his eyes and remembered the rush of power running through him while he was buried to the balls in Emrie. "No, hurt was not the

146

word for it."

His father smiled. "You look happy."

Harrow nodded. "I genuinely am. The search for her was just about to be moved into an earnest examination of my territory, but I am very glad that she simply popped up when she did."

"Ah, yes. What did you do with your other women?"

Harrow shrugged. "They were paid off and escorted to their chosen destination."

His father leaned in. "Do you miss them?"

Harrow chuckled and patted his father's hand. "I do not. I do not miss the fighting, the sniping, or the attempts to lure me into marriage." His smile was slow as he remembered that morning. "Emrie is an exceptional mate. She is not only independent, but she also has a large heart for helping folks achieve their dreams."

"But does she attend to you? I know you have always had... specific needs."

"Yes, Father. She is my match. Lust for lust, but she has no interest in anyone else, nor do I. Our magics and bodies have bonded, and we are right and truly mated."

His father leaned back and grinned. "Excellent. When can I expect grandchildren?"

Harrow blinked. "Demons do not normally produce children."

"Demons do not normally have an equal mating. Your mate is no sobbing girl-child. She has a set to her shoulders that gives off an aura of competence."

"And her curves didn't escape your notice either." Harrow smiled and nodded as one of the servants brought them some weak beer.

"She reminds me of your mother if your mother was two feet taller and built like an ancient shield maiden with ruby eyes." Lord Twell grinned and drank the beer with memories in his gaze.

Harrow knew that he had been exceptionally fortunate in his parents. Their love had been demonstrated as a means to a powerful future. He knew what love looked like at a glance.

Love looked like Emrie.

Chapter Eleven

Emrie finally escaped Murian by heading into the gardens and looking over the collection of blooming flowers. Some herbs got stronger in daylight.

She walked down the paths, and her view kept going to the field just beyond the gardens. It was so close, but there was nothing cultivated there.

Tyda followed her and read out some of the invitations and requests she had been getting.

"Demon Lord Doryn is requesting your help in finding his mate when the time comes. He does not want her raised in his household, he wishes her to be raised in yours."

"Interesting. I will consider it when she appears."

"Very good. The witch kings wish to open a dialogue with you and would like you to accept their envoy."

"Not at present. I am still settling in. I will dictate a letter later."

"Excellent. Now, I have a letter of congratulations from the dragon emperor. He is amused that Lord Harrow has finally found his mate, and he wishes you felicity in your union."

"That sounds pleasant."

Tyda's voice was tense. "Don't be so sure. I was sold to the demon lords by my family. My father died, and my uncle sold me. It is customary for women to revert to their mother's family, and if that family can get rid of an unwanted daughter, they do."

"That is horrible. I will wait on my reply to that one. I am going to have to take things slow. Nothing from the wizards?"

"No, but the vampires are offering you a retainer to assist you."

An idea rushed through Emrie's head. It was barely a thought, but she could see the potential in it. "Oh. This is good."

She whirled toward the stronghold and found Harrow. "Oh, excuse me, Tyda. I will be right back."

She ran into the stronghold and through the halls, past the servants, and up to the upper level where Harrow was looking over his domain with his parents.

"Harrow, I found it!" She ran to him and collided heavily, sending him back a few feet. They weren't near the edge, so that was nice.

"What? What were you looking for?" He was amused by her expression.

"I was looking for something to keep me out of trouble, and I found it." She bit her lip as she smiled. "I need a school."

He wrapped his arms around her waist and widened his grip until it was sliding over her hips.

"What kind of a school?"

She smiled up at him. "A Bride School. A school where women of power can come to be trained to actually be whole people before they let their mates find them. I have enough basic skills to get things started, but I will need to hire teachers."

He leaned down and kissed her lips softly. "What kind of teachers?"

"Magic, music, math, geography, cartography, ceramics, cooking, dance, flower arranging, and healing." She gave him a soft kiss between each of the words.

"Sex?"

"It will be discussed, and they can ask anything they need, but I am not having sex with my students." She nipped his lower lip with her teeth.

He chuckled and tightened his grip. "Hold on."

He lifted her, took a few steps, and dropped off the top of the stronghold, beating his wings to keep them over the rooftops, but soon, they were gliding toward the meadow that she had in mind.

He circled it slowly and brought them in for a surprisingly smooth landing.

"I thought you couldn't fly." She chuckled.

"I can't, but I did mention that I could glide. Now, sex?"

She laughed and reached down for the edge of his skirt. She slid it upward, and his cock sprang out of hiding. The darker skin of his erection was nearly black, and it throbbed when she gripped it. She used her free hand to pull the front of her long tunic and flick it aside. Emrie glanced up at Harrow, and he lifted her against him until the fat, weeping head was pressing into her. She shivered and clutched his shoulders.

He supported her with one hand and peeled her tunic off her shoulders with the other. When her breasts were exposed to his gaze, he didn't hesitate. He scored her nipples lightly in turn, and the rush of moisture that she produced at the hint of pleasurable pain was his indication to proceed.

He thrust in, gripping her hips and pulling her downward. She held onto his arms and wrapped her legs around him while he continued to suck and pull at her breasts. Their coupling was fierce, intense, and she felt the delicate ache that preceded the roar of release.

She whimpered for him to slow, but he took her over the edge and joined her with a roar.

Her pulse thundered in her ears and between her thighs. Her body continued to clasp him with a strong milking motion that made him shudder as his body was coaxed to give its all.

Harrow pressed his forehead against her neck, and she wrapped her arms around his head, running her fingers through his hair.

He slowly raised his head. "How many students?"

"I think that a maximum of sixty would be the target. To start, perhaps six. We would provide everything for them."

He nodded and slowly straightened back to full height. He was still hard inside her, but that was the curse of being a demon king, he was always hard. It made spontaneous sex easy, but his current uniform of a wrap rather awkward in a high wind.

"I wish I could stay inside you for the rest of eternity."

She kissed him sweetly. "Twenty-five percent of your day can be spent within me but not when I am teaching classes or with patients."

"Deal. Yes, you can have your school. They can start on it as soon as I get the artisans together, and I may give it a little assistance."

He rocked his hips against her again, and he looked around. "My privacy screen is holding; shall we seal the deal?"

She gasped and held on as he knelt and proceeded to kiss her neck, breasts, and the inside of her wrists. Harrow occasionally used his teeth but only when he wanted to make her jump.

Inside her, his cock rubbed and shifted as he moved. He bent her back nearly double so that he would not lose his contact inside her, and when she was twisting and pulling at his horns, he pulled back and thrust deep.

She hung on to him and rocked until her limbs were shaking and her clit was approaching agony. Her scream scared birds for miles, and her demon's roar echoed her expression.

They lay locked together, limbs tangled until Emrie heard a polite cough.

"Yes, Tyda?" Her voice was hoarse. Harrow was giving her a very satisfied smile.

"About the wizard contingent?"

"Yes, Tyda?"

Tyda coughed again. "They are here."

"Well, I hope they have had an eyeful."

"They cannot see you through this barrier, but you were very audible. I believe their apprentices are rather sheltered."

Emrie sighed. "I really want to just hit the baths right now."

"That is fine. They can join you there. They need to bathe, frankly." Tyda's disdain was apparent in her voice.

Harrow smirked. "Would you like

some help in rising?"

"Yes, please." False bravado wouldn't change the fact that she had to be physically off Harrow for her body to properly recover.

He rose to his feet, and to her embarrassment, he carried her.

To her surprise, he wrapped her in his wings, concealing her from prying eyes. "Tyda, bring a change of clothing to the baths for me, please. Then, you can bring the wizards to the baths."

"Yes, my lady."

Tyda had seen them locked together before. After the first time, she just smiled.

"This particular position lacks dignity."

"Yes, but it feels delightful."

She remembered something. "Did I take you away from your parents?"

"I took us away. My parents have seen that particular behaviour before."

"Ah. Right. You have always been one for the ladies." She was nestled comfortably against his chest.

"I was only practicing for you, my Queen."

She felt relief when the moisture of the baths surrounded them. "Okay. Time to get down."

He sighed. "Fine. I hope that there will be an entire day where we can just be together for twenty-four hours."

Emrie held onto him as she levered herself away from him and got her balance. She gave him a dark look. "That was Monday. You made Jamis get us snacks."

He grinned. "Yes, but that is the past, I am looking forward."

She laughed and ditched her clothing, easing into what had become her favourite pool. It was just deep enough for her to stand in and her head was still above water.

"You didn't tie your hair up."

She grimaced. "Damn it. Ah well, there is probably grass in it."

He grinned. "And I think there is a small turtle in it as well."

She snorted and went to loosen her braids. When the small turtle popped out, she caught it and set it on the edge of the pools.

When Tyda came to her with the folded clothing, she got her to take the turtle to safety. It had seen more than enough for one day.

Harrow entered the pool with a splash, and he crouched so that his head, wings, and horns were under the water for a moment.

He stood up, and the water was at mid-chest. He was far more imposing than he had been at their first meeting. It was all of the magic that they shared.

She dunked her own head and stood before moving to the edge and taking a seat. Harrow joined her, and they were sitting and cuddling when the wizards walked in.

Emrie kept her mouth shut as the wizards nervously disrobed. They got even warier when the bath attendants came to take their clothing.

Harrow smiled. "They are just going to wash them. If you are not comfortable sharing our bathing area, there are pools nearby. We may converse comfortably."

The eldest of the contingent had silver hair with emerald eyes, and the other two had a more watery green. All of them were constructed of shades of green and grey.

The elder cleared his throat. "It would be an honour to share your bath, my lord."

He stepped into the pool, and his companions followed suit. They quickly swam over to the edge and sat.

Emrie had to ask, "Dearest, how tall

am I?"

"You put most of the warriors I have seen to shame, my Queen."

"Thank you, dearest."

The emissary cleared his throat. "Lord Harrow, I bring greetings from King Minyot. Congratulations on finding your mate."

Emrie saw at once that the wizards were dismissing her as an accessory. This was going to be fun.

"Emissary Liden. She is far more than my mate. She is my queen."

Emrie tried to look shy and demure. She glanced up at Harrow, and he gave a small snort.

"She is also queen of this territory, so all congratulations should go to her for snagging such a willing specimen as myself."

Emrie rolled her eyes, and then, she met the gazes of the wizards.

"Greetings from our demesne to King

Minyot. I hope these words find him well."

The eyes of the young man on the left turned a hot green. Someone was looking through his eyes.

"Harrow, it is good to see you. You are looking well." The voice did not belong to the boy.

Harrow inclined his head. "Minyot. I see you are still working with watered-down wizards."

"It can't be helped. My wife did not give me a child. I am looking for my successor. I will not allow my good works to fall into unworthy hands."

"A sound strategy. This is my mate, Emrie. Emrie, this is the voice and gaze of King Minyot."

"Greetings, Minyot."

The green eyes flared. "Insolent. You should teach her manners, Harrow."

"Honest. I am honest. Harrow can teach me many things, but as you dispensed with the formalities to my mate, I dispensed with them to you." She could tell her eyes were hot. The wizards were nervous.

The channelling wizard paused, and he blinked slowly. A slight nod came from him. "You are correct, my lady. I apologize."

"Accepted under one condition."

"What is that?"

"I need a female instructor to teach magic females the way of wizards."

Harrow laughed, the emissary gasped, and the other young wizard sat with his mouth open.

"We do not teach our women magic."

Emrie nodded. "I knew that when you said your wife did not give you a child. If she had been able to become all she was meant to be, she would have had the ability to match you magic for magic. Then, a child would have come into an equal arrangement. It is awkward, but the demon queens have researched it. When the queen has power, there are heirs."

Every male in the bath was staring at her. The king began to quiz her in earnest, and she answered until her fingers were getting puckered. She called a halt. "I will wish you good day, King Minyot. I am going to check on my assistant. She is working on shadow walking today."

She exited the bath, and there was silence. Tyda appeared from the shadows and handed her drying cloths before picking up her clean clothing and escorting her to the changing area.

The men were speaking heatedly the moment she left, and she knew very well what it was about.

* * * *

"How can there be another demoness in a demon queen's home? It does not

166

happen."

Harrow shrugged. "Perhaps it is because my wife made her a demon. She was slated to be one of my concubines, but she was just too young. She didn't appeal, but I bought her to keep her clear of others with a less scrupulous attitude."

The page stammered. "She. Made. A. Demon."

"Three in total. Two are here, and one has a demesne of his own. She overcharged him. He turned a deep plum colour." Harrow was smirking. He knew it. This was too funny. Minyot was such a superior ass.

"The new lord that took over Dorf's lands."

Harrow cackled. The name spell had spread that far. Impressive.

"Yes. Doryn. The new lord who took it over. He is loyal and has enough power to wrestle the mountain king himself."

"Has your woman given you any of that power?"

Harrow got to his feet and flexed his wings. "You could say that."

He excused himself as the others stared. Unlike Emrie, he had not thought to ask an assistant to prepare clothing for him.

Emrie walked back into the baths, dressed and elegant. She held a folded skirt for him and presented it to him with a bow.

He took it with a smile and laughed at her parting words.

"Cover that up, it's mine."

He left the wizards to recover from their spluttering. His grin was fixed on his face. With a woman like this, his parents might have a grandchild after all.

Epilogue

They stood at the top of the stronghold and looked out over the new construction.

Harrow nuzzled her neck, and she reached up and held one of his horns while she went up on her toes.

"Thank you, Harrow. This is just what I needed."

He spoke against her neck. "This dalliance in the moonlight?"

"It is daylight, my dearest. My King." She chuckled and turned in his arms.

He smiled down at her with his eyes aflame. "You glow and darken the world around you wherever you are. It is what I first noticed about you."

"You noticed my aura? How sweet." She moved closer to him and wrapped her arms around his neck. "I noticed your chest and shoulders and kept going lower from there."

Their kiss was sweet, and before it got hot and heavy, Emrie pulled back. "Thank you, Harrow. This feels right."

He wrapped his wings forward and concealed her completely as his hands ran down her back and slid under the slit in her tunic. "You have always felt right, my dearest."

She giggled and surrendered to the comfort of his shadow.

Emrie paced back and forth in the main hall. "Are you sure that the notices went out in every demesne and kingdom?"

"They did. Jamis went to each one and made sure. Be easy. Today is the first day, after all." Tyda smiled and remained stationary next to the main doors.

"I just... I mean... this is the sort of thing that the families who took me in would have dreamed of. The danger that my presence put them in was a constant worry." Emrie wanted to bite her nails.

"They will come. Jamis has put up over two hundred of the signs across the expanse of the known territories. They will come, and when they do, we will be here."

Emrie paused, and she sighed. "I don't know what I was expecting. I mean, this would be wasted if there were no girls who needed refuge and an education."

"My lady, come, and I will fix you a cup of tea."

Emrie sighed and looked down at her first apprentice. "That sounds surprisingly nice. Let's inspect the kitchens again."

They had just turned to walk to the back of the building when the doors creaked open. Emrie smelled blood, fear, and pain as it stumbled through her doorway and fell to the floor.

Emrie ran to her side and eased her over, looking into eyes so blue it was almost painful. Split lips parted, and on a whisper of words, the girl said, "Is this it? Am I safe?"

Emrie lifted her and walked purposefully to the clinic that she had installed near the entrance for just this purpose. "This is the Bride School, and you are safe."

The young woman collapsed, and her blood-matted hair fell over Emrie's arm. The last sound that she made before she was in the infirmary was, "Sssafe..."

Emrie blinked away the tears in her eyes and went to work. If this was going to be her first student, she was going to have to survive the night.

The girl was clutching one of the postings that Jamis had been putting up. Just wait until she told Harrow.

Girls and young women of power.

If you can read this, you are invited to a safe place.

The Bride School will educate you free of charge in magic, medicine, and all that you need to run your household and your lives.

First, you will be taught to be strong women, and then, you will learn how to be a Bride. The choices are yours. Your life is yours. You need only follow this map, and you will be safe.

Welcome and fear not. Your life and safety is our primary concern.

Come, be safe, and learn how to survive.

The page was stained with blood, but the words were the same ones that

Emrie had agonized over. It had worked. A future as a tutor lay before her, and she couldn't wait to share her joy with her mate.

"Tyda, get me some—"

"Water. Yes, my lady."

While Tyda prepped the water, Emrie removed the girl's clothing via the sharp crook of her finger. The girl was covered with punctures, and since the nearest vampire coalition was two hundred miles away, the girl had either run an incredible distance or teleported. Either way, she needed help, and she needed it now.

The main door opened and closed. Emrie looked at her assistant.

"Here is the water, I will get the door." Tyda nodded.

"Good. Call the others. I am getting the feeling that tonight it will be all hands on deck. Go, now."

"Yes, my lady. Congratulations on a

successful start to the school." Tyda's grin was a flash of amusement.

Emrie began to clean the wounds that were bleeding the worst, and when she had done that, she covered her patient in a blanket.

Emrie was mixing a draught to help clotting when a whisper caught her attention.

"Where am I?"

Emrie answered while working. "You are at the Bride School. It is a new establishment designed to help women of power to ease into their own skins, as it were. You are safe, you will be fed and cared for, and if you are ready to go back into the world, you will have the tools to do so."

The voice grew stronger. "What do you want from me?"

"I want you to try. Choose a profession, a skill, or a subject that you are passionate about and focus on it. We can teach almost anything." Emrie finished the draught and put it in a cup.

When she turned to her patient, the girl recoiled. "Demon!"

Emrie inclined her head. "Demoness. Queen Demoness if you wish. But I was once a girl who looked human and wasn't, who had power but no outlet, who was lucky enough to find caretakers who encouraged knowledge. I became a woman before I became a bride and that is an advantage I wish to share."

The girl recoiled. "I don't want a man anywhere near me."

"That is fine, but if you are destined to be a bride, your blood will call your lord when you are ready."

"They took all my blood. It won't be calling anyone. Where did my clothing go?"

Emrie moved toward her with a casual air. "I needed to remove it to get most of the blood off you. I was a healer before I was a demon, so I did not touch you in any inappropriate way. Now, drink this. It will help stop the blood loss."

The girl blinked slowly. "What is it?"

"It is a mixture of herbs that will slow the flow of your blood, you will remain awake, and if you like, I can show you how to make it." She handed the girl the cup and stepped back to sit on the stool near the medication counter.

She spun idly on her chair and waited while the girl drank the draught.

The blood stopped seeping in under a minute. Poor thing, she must have had nothing else in her system.

The door regularly opened and closed for the next six hours, ending up with twelve young ladies of varying ages and all bristling with magic.

Meals were served, a trip to the baths in the lower levels was arranged, and Emrie was smiling so much her face

177

hurt. By the time everyone was treated for their ills and in bed with caretakers watching over them, Emrie was more than ready to return to her king's embrace. The child that had its start within her during the evening deserved for its father to know.

She looked over the girls in their dorm one more time, and she smiled before leaving them for the night. Private rooms would be issued in the morning. Tonight, the comfort of their own kind would let them rest.

Emrie chuckled the entire way from the school to the stronghold, ignoring the demons that were guarding her against every shadow and rampart.

She was in too good a mood to regret her decision to demonize the more elite of Harrow's forces.

When Emrie walked into their chambers, Harrow was waiting in bed for her, naked, on his side, with candles burning all around the room.

"I hear congratulations are in order, my Queen."

She sat at the edge of the bed and pulled off her boots. "Thank you. Jamis did well. They all had the flyer with them. It was wonderful and horrible, all at the same time."

He sat up. "Horrible?"

"The first girl had been abused by vampires. At least six if the marks were any indication. She is resting, but she was covered in blood."

"Is she one of yours?"

She loosened her sash and dropped it to the floor before pulling her long tunic over her head. "Oh, definitely. I am guessing that the indicator came on late, or she would have fought them off. I also think she teleported, so I am guessing witch."

"Is she all right?"

Emrie reached up and stretched while

letting her hair unravel into a living mass around her. "She will be."

Harrow moved to her, and he pulled her across his lap, pinning his erection between them. She grinned at him. "I have other news for you, my King."

He nibbled on her neck. "Did you also get a wizard and a dragon?"

She hissed and leaned into his lips. "Yes, but what I wanted to tell you is that you can begin to work on your landing techniques. Ten months from now, you will be flying."

His head jerked up, and she dodged his horns.

The next hours were spent with him worshipping every inch of her, with special attention paid to her belly. She was sated and happy when he held her in his arms, and feathered kisses over her cheeks, nose, and forehead.

She waited until he was almost asleep, and then, she had to ask the question she was dying to know the answer to. "Did you wax your horns?"

His laughter answered her question, and she looked forward to thousands of nights and days with the joy she was feeling on this one, perfect day, with her destined demon in her arms.

Author's Note

Whew. Now, I know why I shouldn't anime binge during the holidays.

This is going to be a sealed series of four... or five. Let's see, demons, witches, wizards, dragons, so four. Four for now.

So, off for more cartoon heroes and heroines who can be so much more. Since it isn't bee season, I have a lot more time to just keep my head down and go.

Thanks for reading,

Viola Grace

About the Author

$\mathcal{V}$iola Grace (aka Zenina Masters) is a Canadian sci-fi/paranormal romance writer with ambitions to keep writing for the rest of her life. She specializes in short stories because the thrill of discovery, of all those firsts, is what keeps her writing.

An artist who enjoys a story that catches you up, whirls you around, and sets you down with a smile on your face is all she endeavours to be. She prefers to leave the drama to those who are better suited to it, she always goes for the cheap laugh.

In real life, she now is engaged in

beekeeping, and her adventures can be found on the YouTube channel, Mystery Bees Apiary. Just look for the cartoon kittens.

CPSIA information can be obtained
at www.ICGtesting.com
Printed in the USA
BVHW010631070822
643973BV00016B/1240